Praise for **St**

For William

And for Tiger, who sadly left before

this book was finished

This edition first published in the UK in 2024 by Usborne Publishing Limited,
Usborne House, 83-85 Saffron Hill, London EC1N 8RT, England, usborne.com

Usborne Verlag, Usborne Publishing Ltd., Prüfeninger Str. 20,
93049 Regensburg, Deutschland VK Nr. 17560

First published 2024. Text copyright © Shirley Marr, 2024.

The right of Shirley Marr to be identified as the author of this work has been asserted
by her in accordance with the Copyright, Designs and Patents Act, 1988.

Cover illustration by Sian James © Usborne Publishing, 2024.

The name Usborne and the Balloon logo are Trade Marks of
Usborne Publishing Limited.

A CIP catalogue record for this book is available from the British Library.

JFMAMJJASO D/23 ISBN 9781805073628 9542/1

Printed and bound using 100% renewable energy at CPI Group (UK) Ltd, Croydon, CR0 4YY.

MIX
Paper | Supporting
responsible forestry
FSC® C171272
www.fsc.org

SHIRLEY MARR

COUNTDOWN TO YESTERDAY

USBORNE

GO LAUNCH

It seems strange to start a story with a goodbye. But as I sit in the time machine with Tiger on my shoulder, I look over at Yan and for a split second I don't want to go. I want to stay in the present. Because I can see things now, things I couldn't begin to understand two weeks ago. But Yan gives me a thumbs up. She turns the big button on the black box and confirms the coordinates. I go to place my hands over my face because it's overwhelming, but they touch upon the plastic visor of my helmet. I tell myself I'm ready. The lights flicker. There's a low hum in the air. I watch the countdown on all the screens. Time s l o w s and white smoke fills the floor. I squeeze my eyes shut.

Mum announces at dinner that she's going to enter the Summerlake Primary School Cake Competition this year.

I'm shocked at this news.

In the *for ever* that the school's been holding the fundraiser, Mum has entered it a total of...

Zero times.

I should be happy about this news.

"Therefore, James, I'll be walking down to the school with you tomorrow morning," she says.

Dad doesn't say anything, he just cuts up his steak. I don't say anything either. I don't like steak. Mum has made me beef rissoles and I cut one in half.

Every year, parents get to select one of the cakes in *The Australian Women's Weekly Children's Birthday Cake*

Book to bake. And every year, two weeks before my birthday, I'd look slowly through our copy and make a fantasy Top Ten list in my head. I'd wish so hard that Mum would make me a cake. Any cake. I'd even be happy with the worst one – the Hickory Dickory Watch, which features a mouse made out of a large prune. But she never has.

I *am* happy about this news. My brain starts trying to pick which cake I want. Robert Robot. No, the Swimming Pool filled with green jelly. The Cricket Bat with my name piped in the corner.

But I am suspicious.

Mum is obviously trying to make up for something. *Or*, she's guilty of something. *Or*, she's got bad news.

"I've found a house," she suddenly blurts out.

She bursts into tears.

Oh. I guess it's all three.

Dad puts his knife and fork down and stares at his plate. So do I.

I don't want to move again. We moved just last year, and I still consider this place that we're living in right now "the new house".

We've moved five times in total. Dad says it's actually been seven times, but I was too little to remember the first two. That's like once every one-and-a-half years since I was born. The houses all seem exactly the same to me – I don't know what my parents are looking for. Each time we move, my trundle bed loses more bits. The bottom bed that used to be able to slide under the top bed no longer does, so the bedroom door bangs against it.

The last moving man stepped on my mattress and left a black boot print. It doesn't matter which sheets Mum uses to cover it up, I know it's there.

But I tuck my hand into the crook of Mum's arm because I know it comforts her. I shovel down a big spoonful of peas and chew them with my mouth closed, without her telling me to.

Mum pats my fingers. As her crying turns to sniffles, she gets her phone out, even though we have a no-phone policy at the dinner table. She flicks through a whole bunch of photos and shows me. . .

A small, empty bedroom with grey carpet. An even smaller bedroom with the same grey carpet. A kitchenette with one wonky cabinet door. A lime-green bathroom with only a shower cubicle, no bathtub. A concrete balcony. Then, strangely, a photo of a room full of washing machines.

I ask her why she's showing me this and she says that's where we'd be doing our laundry from now on. In the shared room at the bottom of the building. Because the apartment is too small to have its own washing machine.

This blows my mind. I remember when we were on a family holiday to Broome once and Mum had to use a coin-operated clothes dryer at the resort. She decided to clean the lint filter because she's fussy like that. I'm not going to mention what she found inside that lint filter. Mum started storing all our dirty clothes for when we got home. Me and Dad had to hear about it non-stop for the rest of the trip.

So, I don't understand why Mum is now looking at me that way, as though she's hoping for my approval on this house.

"Where is all of Dad's stuff going to fit?" I ask.

And by that, I mean his sixteen computers that run his programming experiments all day and all night, testing strange things like what would happen if the moon fell out of orbit or if the sun exploded. Dad is a Geek Twenty-Four-Seven. He goes to work at the Commonwealth Scientific and Industrial Research Organisation and spends his time with computers, and then he comes home and spends more time with computers just for fun.

There is also his tuba, bassoon and flugelhorn, as complicated and as big as the plumbing under a sink. Although he hasn't played any of them since I was born.

All of it takes up a whole room.

"We don't have to worry about Dad's stuff," says Mum. "Because Dad isn't coming with us."

She bursts into tears again.

I look at Mum with her face in her hands. Sobbing.

I look at Dad, who very calmly says to me, "James, your mother and I have been discussing this for a long time and we've decided on a divorce. We'll be living in different homes and you'll be spending half the week at one and half at the other. It's not an exact science because, as you know, a week has an odd number of days. But that doesn't mean anything has to change."

That's like Dad saying that nothing would change if the earth suddenly rotated in the opposite direction.

It would lead to the end of the world.

I know because Dad showed me on one of his computer simulations. The earth is spinning so fast that, if it suddenly stopped, everything would be hurled hundreds of kilometres forward. People, cars, buildings.

The ocean would slosh like a bowl of water being tossed out. Mountains would break and go shooting off like giant arrowheads.

The only way to avoid this would be if the earth came to a gradual halt first.

But my parents haven't eased me into this news, they've dumped it on me.

Bam! Just like that.

My heart and stomach are now down the street somewhere.

Where was I when they had these "discussions"?

Mum is still crying, and I think about putting my hand back in the crook of her arm, but instead I get out of my chair and I run to my room. I want to slam my door, but I can't because the bottom bed of my broken trundle is in the way. So, disappointingly, I have to push the door closed. It does so with a bang and a scrape. I crawl into the top bed and put the duvet over my head.

I hear my parents talking in the dining room. The sounds of the table being cleared and the kitchen tap running. They must be doing their normal routine – Dad washing and Mum drying. Why are they still pretending everything is the same when it isn't any more?

My bedroom door opens. There's a bang and a scrape when it hits the trundle bed.

Dad comes in and sits on my bed. "Can we talk?" he asks.

I don't reply.

Dad clears his throat. But nothing else comes out because he's only really good at technical speak, not emotional stuff.

After a while he gets up, says, "Hang in there, mate," and closes the door after him.

Mum comes in next and again there's the bang of the door against the trundle bed. "We really need to get that fixed," she says, obviously hoping it's a conversation starter.

It's not.

"I'm going to make the Rocket cake for the competition," says Mum.

That's the most popular cake. Every year all the parents fight over that cake. I don't blame them. It's the tallest cake out of all of them and it's awesome.

"I'll make sure I'm the first parent through that gate tomorrow morning." Her voice quivers.

Tears are rolling down my face, but I keep the duvet over my head so she can't see.

I don't know whether I'm crying because I'm still upset about before or whether it's now replaced by the fact that Mum is going to make the Rocket cake.

"We'll talk about it in the morning. Who knows? In the morning, everything might be wonderful," she suggests.

It won't.

Maybe it'll be wonderful for them because it's what they want. Even though they come into my room individually, it's like they're ganging up on me.

Mum leaves and it's all quiet.

I flick on my night-light, which is a globe. My anger has lost its sharp edges and I wish I didn't feel so alone. I look at the bright outlines of all the countries and continents of planet earth and pretend I'm an astronaut floating out in space.

My duvet rustles softly and I feel Tiger coming to sit on top of my legs. She's not actually a real tiger, but don't upset her by telling her that. She can always tell when anyone in the family is unwell or sad. Dad says her purr is the same frequency as the one scientists use in vibration therapies to heal tissue and bone.

I know I don't have anything broken in me, but it is still a comfort.

THINGS THAT WILL NEVER HAPPEN AGAIN NOW THAT MY PARENTS ARE NOT TOGETHER
#1

Stuck on the back of my bedroom door is a large poster of David Bowie. I was seven years old when I heard a song of his on the radio. I remember because I was obsessed with everything space at the time. It started off about an astronaut called Major Tom who is so famous, everyone wants to know everything about him, including what brand of shirt he wears.

Then, one day in space, he loses contact with Ground Control.

I wish I wasn't listening so closely then.

I don't normally get scared. I mean, as a seven-year-old I could watch the scary bits in cartoons that other kids couldn't take and laugh about it. But this song really messed me up. Major Tom floats out into space all alone after becoming untethered from his spaceship. I couldn't think of a worse way to go.

But Mum and Dad sat down with me because they could see I was upset, and they tried to comfort me in their own way.

Dad, always scientific, said that space was cold and that, eventually, when Major Tom ran out of oxygen, it would be like drifting off to sleep. He probably wouldn't even feel it. He'd be snap frozen, like a bag of peas. Maybe some alien spacecraft would spot him, with his bright orange hair, and pick him up. Who knew what technology the aliens had? Dad believes in aliens. Four of his sixteen computers scan the skies endlessly, looking for intelligent communication.

Mum, on the other hand, always takes a more creative view of things. She printed out the song lyrics at work and we looked through them together when she got home. She said that Major Tom *wanted* to cut himself off from planet earth. That he was sick of humans and their tiresome ways and wanted to be left alone. She thinks he's happy now, doing his own thing.

Sometimes when I can't sleep, I look at David Bowie with his glittery silver space top and his mismatched eyes

and I don't feel like I'm always the odd one out.

I don't even think about what happened to Major Tom any more, instead I think of how Dad and Mum teamed up and stopped me from being scared. Like having a warm sticky date pudding in my belly and the whole world being okay.

Now that they're splitting up, I'll never have that again. That's what scares me.

Mum was serious after all. She wakes me up early the next day so she can be the first through the school gates when they open. So she can be the first parent to put her name down for the Summerlake Primary School Cake Competition.

"How are you feeling, James?" she asks.

"Fine," I grumble and try to go back under the covers because I hate mornings. But she threatens to brush my teeth and change my clothes for me, and I'm reminded that everything Mum says, she follows through with, so I get a move on.

That's how I end up seeing the girl with the X-ray eyes.

Now, I'm not saying she has electrons for eyes, I'm

using what Mum would call an *analogy*. The girl has perfectly normal eyes. It's just what she sees with them.

I watch her walking parallel to us on the other side of the road, which makes no sense because the footpath is on our side. And she's reading a book at the same time. I can't explain how dangerous this is because the street goes down a hill and, even when you're concentrating, a trip means you'd go rolling past at least two houses.

I heard a rumour at school that this one kid pushed another, and that the other kid rolled all the way down. Luckily there happened to be an ambulance at the bottom, because they went to hospital with two broken legs.

The girl bumps right into a power pole. She lowers her book and stares at the pole as if to question why it's there. With the intensity of her stare, she might be able to burn two holes through to the other side.

Then she does something even stranger. She feels all the way around the pole, as if to test that it's actually a real, solid power pole. As we continue walking parallel to each other, I watch her part the leaves on a bush and look into it.

Maybe she heard a bird or a cat hidden inside. It looks

more to me like she's questioning whether the bush is what it seems.

I shake my head and stop paying attention to her, as we are now almost up to the school gates.

And we're the first ones there!

Mum is so proud of this she is doing fist pumps. Then she kicks a high-heeled boot into the air. I try to hide inside my school fleece jacket. Luckily there's no one to see.

Well, no one except for the girl with the X-ray eyes. She lines up behind us, still reading her book.

I look at the title. *The Essential 1983 Guide for the Serious Use of the BBC Micro Computer!*

I have no idea why she is reading something from over forty years ago. That computer would have less memory than the kind of free USB stick Dad gets from conferences and then forgets all about in a drawer.

She notices me looking at her, stuffs the book into her bag and stares long and hard at me. The tips of my ears get hot enough to fry an egg on.

"The algorithm is different today," she announces.

That is honestly the first thing that comes out of her mouth.

"I'm always the first person to the gate," she continues, as if I need an explanation. "I wait for two minutes and then Mrs Tagliatelle opens the gate and lets me in."

She blows hot air onto her knitted gloves, the kind with the fingertips missing, and waits for me to reply.

I don't say anything.

She starts counting down from ten quietly under her breath. I kick my restless legs and hover around Mum, who is busy glued to her phone like a regular adult.

"Now," the girl whispers.

As if on cue, Mrs Tagliatelle, the admin lady, comes to open the gate. Mum waves. Mrs Tagliatelle looks very surprised to see Mum there.

"Everything has changed. Sometimes all it takes is one variable," the girl says, as if she's surprising herself. "I'm Yan, by the way."

I should say hi back. Yan is Chinese, like my mum, and Mum thinks politeness is a virtue. Sometimes she'll talk about manners and honour and her eyes will get that faraway look, as if she's looking back at things from a long time ago, even before she was born. But Dad isn't Chinese so Mum's not strict about any of this stuff.

I don't get a chance anyway, as Mum is already

impatiently hurrying me through the gate, following Mrs Tagliatelle. Yan follows us for a while, until she turns left towards the library.

"I'll see you around, James Greenaway. It's a real shame we're not in the same class. Maybe next year."

I didn't tell her my name.

I guess she's heard some of those schoolyard stories about me.

Just my luck.

Yan knocks three times on the library door and peers through the frosted glass panel.

I'm curious to see what happens next, but I get dragged to the front office.

"I'm here to enter the cake competition!" Mum declares, a little too loudly.

"Your first time, huh?" says Mrs Tagliatelle. "Welcome to our world of butter cream and fluffy frosting; where liquorice allsorts can be used to make anything from a gutter on a log cabin to eyelashes for sharks."

"I've decided this will be a year of *firsts*," replies Mum and my stomach sinks.

A year where Mum walks away from our house and never comes back.

"Which cake will it be, love?" asks Mrs Tagliatelle.

Laid out on a dedicated table is a special card for each of the cakes from *The Australian Women's Weekly Children's Birthday Cake Book*. An excited *zing!* goes right through me knowing I helped make those cards.

This year, Mrs Tagliatelle has even decorated the table with a crêpe paper skirt and made a special badge for herself that reads *Cake Coordinator*. Since I've been helping for over two years now, she's made one for me with *Cake Committee* on it. Which I do wear.

Sometimes.

It's not like the kids in class would make fun of me or anything.

The competition gets bigger and better every year. It started out as another fundraiser for the school, along with the Lamington Drive, Rope Jump and the Colour Run Carnival, but it's now become the event of the year. Sure, parents like seeing their kids winning over other kids. But when they get their own special contest, they like seeing themselves win over other parents more. Especially when the winner gets to go onstage and receive a golden apron in front of everyone else.

Mum pretends to politely look at the other cards and

lingers on Cuddly Koala, Good Witch and the Piano. But Mum is acting like an overexcited kid. I can already tell which one she's going to pick.

"The Rocket cake, please," says Mum confidently.

Mrs Tagliatelle lifts her eyebrows. "I have to give the warning every year that it's one of our most difficult cakes," she says. "Even for experienced bakers. Perhaps a nice and simple cake to choose would be the Number One. You just need a sharp knife and a packet of Smarties."

"It has to be the Rocket cake," repeats Mum and she looks over at me.

I can see she's trying so hard, and I want to smile back for her, but I can't find it in me. If I smile, I'll start crying.

"That'll be a five-dollar entry fee, please."

Mum passes over the money and rubs her hands in excitement.

Mrs Tagliatelle presents her with the card in a solemn fashion. "It's always the height of the cake that's the downfall for the baker," she advises. "On top of that, this incredibly tall cake has to balance on cardboard boosters. You can talk about *blast-offs* all you want, but boy, have I seen some *splats* in past years!"

Mrs Tagliatelle laughs at her own joke. Mum laughs

too. I stand there and get embarrassed about old-people humour.

"I'd better get going to work now…" Mum trails off and looks like she doesn't want to go to work at all. "I'll see you after school, James."

I give Mum a cool nod and, gripping the card tightly in her hand, she hurries out of the office.

"Your mum loves you," says Mrs Tagliatelle. "You know that, don't you?"

She gives me a deliberate glance before getting out the Cake Entry Book, so caked and encrusted in frosting it looks like an ancient artefact. On a fresh page she writes *Rocket cake – Sophie Koh.*

"I'm sorry, but you've got her surname wrong," I point out. "My mum's name is *Sophie Greenaway.*"

Mrs Tagliatelle stops and gives me that look.

The look that adults give kids when they feel sorry for them.

"Love, I thought you knew about, you know…*your parents.*"

"Of course I know," I say too loudly. I'm heading out the door so fast I'm running.

It never occurred to me that Mum would revert back

to her unmarried name. I thought she'd keep the surname Greenaway because it's all I've ever known her as and it's the name everyone else knows her by too. But obviously she had a life before she had me. Before she married Dad.

Now we're no longer connected by the same last name. It's like I'm drifting even further away from her, like she's Ground Control and I'm Major Tom.

Yan is standing outside the library, almost as if she's waiting for me.

"I saw your mum go past with one of those cake cards," she informs me, looking up from her book. "Is it the Typewriter cake? That one is my favourite. All those Smarties for keys."

"Then get your own mum to make it for you!" I shout at her for no reason.

"I wish she would, but she says that's something only Australian mums do." Yan looks a little sad. "Which makes me wonder if I'm Australian."

I don't know what on earth she's talking about. She sounds Australian to me.

Even though I should turn around and apologize to her, I want to run off somewhere. Somewhere I won't be found.

But all I can do is go to class.

THINGS THAT WILL NEVER HAPPEN AGAIN NOW THAT MY PARENTS ARE NOT TOGETHER

#2

You should have seen the cake I got last year for my birthday. It was an entire space-scape and it was *huge*. With a rocket ship and a spaceman and this weird bumpy surface of a planet with aliens hiding in the craters. It was made by a designer bakery that has thousands of followers on social media.

Mum had promised that she was going to bake my cake herself. I had started looking through *The Australian Women's Weekly Children's Birthday Cake Book* in preparation, in case it wasn't going to be a surprise and she wanted me to choose. I was leaning hard towards the Blackboard cake because, in the book, the writing on it reads: *Happy birthday Jamie*. But for some reason she didn't end up making a cake at all and ordered it instead.

She showed me how the House of Flake & Crumble had put a picture of my cake online, where it had received one thousand and twenty-two likes, including some heart emojis from a local celebrity who had been on a popular reality baking show, so it's not like I could be disappointed or anything.

It was probably for the best. I remember when one of the school dads made the *Women's Weekly* Echidna ice-cream cake with chocolate biscuit sticks for spikes and a set of lolly teeth and put it on social media.

It got hundreds of comments. . .

Making fun of it.

To be honest it really did look like something out of a nightmare, especially the teeth. I shudder when I think of the teeth.

"Which bit is the cake...as in the part you can eat?" I'd asked, looking at the space cake.

"You can eat all of it. Every single bit," Mum answered.

Everything was made of mouldable icing and sugar. Even the spaceman, which I thought was a toy figurine. How awesome is that?

The wind had blown right then, lifting the plastic tablecloth on the trestle table. The cake didn't even move.

That's how heavy it was.

You should have seen the kids' faces when they saw the cake. Well, Cousin Jackson and Cousin Harry's faces anyway, because the kids I invited from school didn't show up. It might have been mass gastro or flu or something because Mum made me invite everyone, including my arch-nemesis Roscoe Stonecutter.

Me and my cousins stared at the cake and eventually Mum and Dad came over too and put their arms over all of us in a group hug.

"What do you think?" Mum asked.

"It's the best cake," I replied, after seeing my cousins' faces.

"Can we start on the food now?" asked Jackson, searching around for his parents. They are both Chinese and are quite strict. I've been to their place for dinner and you get told when you can eat, you don't ask.

"Of course," replied Dad, and we started shovelling all the party food I had requested onto paper plates. Fried vermicelli noodles, curry puffs and spring rolls. But also, sausage rolls, party pies and honey joys. The best from both of Mum and Dad's worlds.

There was *so* much food. Mum had catered for twenty

kids. Me and my cousins ate and ate until we were so full. We couldn't even jump on the trampoline; we just lay flat on it.

Now that Mum and Dad are splitting up, are they going to hold individual birthday parties for me? And what are the chances of the kids at school coming to two birthday parties when I can't get them to come to one? It'll become too hard. And hard things always get abandoned. Left to one side. Forgotten. Or thrown out like a kerbside rubbish collection.

2 WEEKS 4 DAYS
2 HOURS 0 MINUTES
UNTIL GO LAUNCH

Normally, both my parents trust me to walk home by myself while they're at work.

Even if they aren't at work, neither of them likes the idea of picking me up at "Hectic Hour", when parents with cars jam up the whole street, and parents with prams, strollers, toddlers and dogs weave precariously in between.

But at 3pm, as we all spill out of class after the bell has sounded, I can see Mum standing at the open gate in the middle of the other parents, waving and smiling at me.

She shouts, "Hurry up before the inspector arrives! I'm sure I'm illegally parked!"

For some reason, I search for Yan. But she's not there.

I take Mum's hand, because she offers it to me. Even though I'm too old. I stare at the ground, as if not being able to see my classmates means they can't see me.

On the other side of the road, in a spot that is clearly marked *Keep Clear at All Times*, *$500 fine*, is Mum's Corolla.

With a trailer hitched to the back.

Mum waves happily at the line of honking cars stuck behind her and gets in. I have to sit in the back because Helga, our large house plant, is in the front passenger seat. I turn to look out the rear window and I can see the trailer stacked with a bedside drawer, a plastic trestle table, four stools, a cube storage case and Mum's favourite reading chair. Next to me is Mum's huge overnight bag with the flamingo print.

"Where are we going?" I ask as she drives off in the opposite direction of home.

"You're helping me to move in today! No time like the present, right?" Mum's voice is so bright and bubbly I get suspicious. But she has this big smile on her face that looks genuine, like she's happy.

Mum pulls up to an old apartment complex and presses a clicker. A green metal gate opens with a horrible screech and then closes with the same horrible screech once we've driven through. She points to where her designated parking spot is (number 51), but because she

y

32

has the trailer, she parks right outside the entrance in a spot that reads *Loading Zone Only, Wheel Clamping Without Warning.*

"Help me with the reading chair, won't you, Treasure?" asks Mum.

I blush and look around. I know Mum has called me that since I was born, and that my middle name is the Chinese word for treasure, but I'm eleven years old now. Luckily, there is no one around.

I help Mum lift and pile all the things from the trailer next to the lift, and we take Helga up first. The lift smells disgusting, like one of those yellow deodorizing cakes they put in the school toilets. The door to her apartment is the kind where you have to turn the key and the handle at the same time. Mum turns the key and I turn the handle, Mum only having one hand as she's holding Helga like a baby.

"This place is a little old," explains Mum, as though I expected the door to be controlled by a keyless electronic touchpad. "But it's the only thing I could find on such short notice. I'll find something nicer in time."

Mum really couldn't wait to leave, I think glumly, as she reminds me to remove my shoes. She makes it sound as though it was unbearable at home when actually, everything was fine.

Until last night.

The apartment looks exactly like Mum had showed me, but in real life it also feels depressing. I guess you can't feel emotions through photos.

"Let me give you a tour," says Mum.

She shows me all the rooms. It doesn't take very long, because the place is small. The other thing about photos is that you can't smell them. In real life the bathroom has a mouldy pong and the carpets have a faint wet dog stink.

"It just needs a few drops of essential oil and a good vacuum," Mum suggests.

The kitchen looks smaller in real life, if that is even possible.

I don't understand why she seems okay about moving to this place from our nice weatherboard house.

Mum opens the oven. She says she's never used a gas one before and wonders if it might suddenly "explode". She thinks she needs to manually stick a BBQ lighter inside to get it going. Combined with Mum's capacity to freak out about household appliances, like that time at the laundromat in Broome, the chances of her baking anything in it are slim.

Yet, determinedly stuck on the wonky kitchen cabinet door is the card with *Rocket cake* written on it.

The two bedrooms with the grey carpet – one small and the other smaller – are exactly as they are in the photos. Mum says I can have the bigger room and I don't say no.

We end the tour on the concrete balcony. Mum optimistically says she's going to put two chairs there, so we can sit and watch the sunset, even though the space barely holds the two of us standing side by side.

"Look at this million-dollar view!" exclaims Mum. "The rent is an absolute steal."

I scan the view and from here I can see my school. I can also see the hill and, at the top of it, our home.

Do I still call it *our home*? Or do I now call it *Me and Dad's Home*? Or the *Old Home*? Thinking about it gives me a funny feeling that I don't have a name for. A little bit like anxiety and sadness and dread all rolled into one, but not exactly any of those things individually.

"What do you think, James?" asks Mum. "I can't wait to do this place up!"

"How come you moved out instead of Dad?" I blurt

out, aware that my voice is very squeaky.

"You have to understand, James," replies Mum, which often means she's about to say something I won't understand. "When I first met your father, I was still living with my family. I went straight from living at home to living with someone else and then getting married and having you. I've always wondered what it would be like to have a place I chose all by myself."

I'm right. I don't understand at all.

Mum makes it sound like getting married was a horrible thing.

I look back at the hill.

Maybe I will call it *House on the Hill.* That sounds neutral. Like it's just another house with no meaning or memory.

"Let's go back downstairs and collect the rest of my things," says Mum. "In case anyone takes them. Not that I want you to think this building is like that or anything. . ."

It's weird that Mum is even using the words "my things" when some of those things my parents had bought together. Like the reading chair and the storage cube. Definitely the bedside drawer, because it is part of a pair. Mum has taken the one from her side of the bed.

"I'm going to drive you back home – whoops!" says Mum and makes her sorry-I-didn't-mean-to-say-that face. "I mean to *your father's place.*"

"Can I please stay with you?" I ask.

It comes out sounding like I'm begging, but I'm not.

"No, treasure. It isn't quite set up properly yet," she replies. "There's no bed. Or more importantly, a kettle to make a cuppa! Even *I'm* not going to stay here tonight. I'm going to a hotel."

I want to ask Mum why she doesn't stay back at the House on the Hill for the night. But I guess that goes against the point of her moving out.

2 WEEKS 3 DAYS
19 HOURS 0 MINUTES
UNTIL GO LAUNCH

For the first time ever, me and Dad are alone in the house.

Dad doesn't quite know what he's supposed to do. He orders a home-delivered pizza – Hawaiian, my favourite – but it doesn't taste as good as it normally does. I blame it on the crust; I swear they've changed the recipe.

We eat together on the couch and afterwards Dad tries to watch his favourite show – about two European detectives who stand around in the dark having long conversations and trying to solve a murder that seems to take for ever, even though the town only has, like, six people in it – but he says he can't concentrate and switches the TV off.

Even then, he keeps picking up his phone, staring at it and putting it back down. Eventually, he stands up and trudges to each of the rooms where Mum has taken furniture away. He stares at the empty spaces. He ends up in the bedroom, staring at the one remaining bedside drawer. With a heavy sigh, he sits down on the mattress, on Mum's side, and looks down at the square of flattened carpet the other one left behind.

I follow him around the house, feeling as useful as a piece of space junk floating around the orbit of earth.

Tiger slinks into the room and stares at Dad. The fur on her back bristles and she shoots out of the room like a comet. Mum says animals can detect bad emotional vibrations. Dad says *bad emotional vibrations* is not a scientific term.

I worry for Tiger because all three of us chose her at the Cat Haven. Or should I say she chose us. Tiger cannot be split into two like furniture. Tiger also can't be expected to go between two houses like me.

I get frightened because Dad's never this quiet. He's always talking about some new experiment he's got his sixteen computers doing or some bizarre fact about his kitchen sink brass instruments – like if you stretched out the tubing of a trumpet it would be 1.98 metres long, taller than most adults.

Leaving Dad in the room by himself, I go and sit on my own bed, stare at the poster of David Bowie and wonder if Dad's computers would be able to calculate the odds of the distance between me and Dad and Mum ever closing up again.

Miss Babette doesn't believe that the desks in class should be in rows, so she arranges them in a big wonky rectangle, open at one end. She doesn't like the idea of all the students staring at her and thinking she's always in the right. She also thinks it's better if we "face our peers". It just makes looking at the whiteboard really hard, especially if you're sitting side-on.

She also doesn't like us sitting next to the same person all the time, something about "getting to know our peers", so every day she will rotate the nametags on our desks. Coming in each morning is like a lottery.

And sometimes you get the booby prize.

I have to sit next to Roscoe Stonecutter today. I thought it was bad when I had to sit opposite him yesterday and he threw a spitball at me. But I have to try to be friends with Roscoe because our mums are best friends. Even though they don't *behave* like best friends, as Mrs Stonecutter is so mean to Mum. But Mum says they have known each other since primary school and that is something worth holding onto. That friendships are complicated, that I'll understand when I'm an adult. I'm not convinced.

All I know is that, earlier this year, Mrs Stonecutter came over for a visit because she hadn't seen this sixth house we'd moved into yet. She asked what was in the big back room. Mum said it was Dad's Man Cave and sounded quite proud of it, actually. Mrs Stonecutter asked why Dad had a Man Cave, and Mum said she believes Dad deserves his own space.

Well, do you have a Woman Cave then? asked Mrs Stonecutter, and Mum said *no*. I'm sure that had nothing to do with Mum moving out. She never said anything about it afterwards. But maybe it made Mum think about why she didn't have a room for her hobbies, even though Mum doesn't really have a hobby. Mrs Stonecutter had said that if it were *her* home, she would turn the Man Cave into a guest room or a home gym instead.

Meanwhile, Roscoe – who had also come over that day – went into my bedroom without permission and made fun of my David Bowie poster. He asked me why I had a clown on the back of my door. I said he wasn't a clown, he was a *spaceman*, but Roscoe didn't listen, and I could tell he'd made up his mind to be mean.

Miss Babette asks us to please sit down. She wants to start class by announcing the theme for Science Week this year, which is *Vehicles of the Future*. The class perks up and I get a bit excited too. It's cool. Last year's theme was fruit and vegetables, which had some suspicious agenda behind it, if you ask me.

All the classes are assigned something different and our project is to make posters for a display in the library. It sounds boring, but at least it won't be "exciting" like last year when the experiment was to make dyes out of different vegetables. Let's just say it's not pleasant boiling purple cabbage, Brussels sprouts or chillies. Especially if you have nostrils.

Our teacher continues and tells us we shouldn't think about the theme as being only about cars. For example, NASA are trying to figure out how to build an elevator that goes to the moon. They've even got a one-million-dollar prize for the first person to invent it.

I'm proud that I've heard about the space elevator before. Dad built a simulation of it on one of his computers. I said we could be rich with that one million dollars, but he got self-conscious and said it was only hypothetical. That some things sound great in theory, but never work out in reality.

Roscoe says really loudly that he's going to do his poster on cars that run on methane gas and then he makes fart noises with his armpit when Miss Babette isn't paying attention. I give him a look, but he doesn't seem to care.

At lunchtime, I go to the front office and ask Mrs Tagliatelle if she has any jobs she wants me to help with, such as photocopying or looking at the school newsletter before it gets emailed, because I'm really good at spelling and grammar. Last time I picked up two words that needed apostrophes and one obviously misspelt word, and Mrs Tagliatelle said *great job*.

I make sure I'm wearing my *Cake Committee* badge and check out the dedicated table for the cake contest as soon as I get there. All the cards are gone already except for three. I straighten the remaining cards, so they look neat. Admire the borders, which feature slices of cakes with sprinkles, a special stationery order just for the competition.

Mrs Tagliatelle is busy answering the phone that won't stop ringing. She asks if I can be a pet and stand by the table in case any more parents arrive. A man in a sharp business suit comes in, still talking on the phone. He stares at the table. I stand up straight and put my hands behind my back.

He covers the speaker on his phone and says, "Which one would you choose?"

"The Candy Castle," I say without hesitation. "You only need a square cake and four upside-down ice-cream cones to make turrets. The icing and decorations are all up to you. You can use Smarties because that's traditional, but if you don't like Smarties, you can use Skittles. It's not in the book, but last year the contestant made a drawbridge out of cream wafers and it looked awesome."

The man, still talking on the phone, nods and holds out a five-dollar note rolled between his fingers. I pass the card to him. I get him to write down his name next to

Candy Castle in the record book. He doesn't ask me why I know so much about the cakes and he doesn't say thanks.

There are only two cards left.

That's when Mrs Stonecutter comes in. She's wearing her gym gear, carrying grizzly Baby Violet on her hip.

"What are you doing here, James?" she says to me in an accusing voice.

"I'm helping out. Mrs Tagliatelle says I can." I look over my shoulder towards the reception desk.

"You should be outside," Mrs Stonecutter complains. "Getting some fresh air, kicking a ball around and doing sports. Like Roscoe."

I don't like sports. I'm not very coordinated. I'm better at stuff like picking up words missing their apostrophes or ones that are obviously misspelt. But I don't bother telling that to Mrs Stonecutter.

She looks at the remaining cards on the table and gets really grumpy.

"I guess the Rocket cake is taken, then? I can't believe there are only two cakes left! The White Rabbit one needs to be covered in desiccated coconut and that's going to go everywhere! And the Stove is even worse! As if I have time to go out and try to find the plastic pots and pans that go on top!"

I want to tell Mrs Stonecutter that if she wanted the Rocket cake she should have come *earlier*. Like *yesterday*. *In the morning*. Before the other parents woke up.

Anyway, the competition is supposed to be fun. She doesn't have to enter if she doesn't want to.

But I don't say these things because it will just make Mrs Stonecutter go ballistic. Adults don't like to hear things from kids. They call that being a *smart alec*.

Although it appears to be all right for adults to say whatever they want back to kids.

"I'll take the Stove, then," says Mrs Stonecutter, even though she had just said it was worse than the White Rabbit. She stares at me and I stare back.

"Well?" she says. "Are you going to give me the card or not?"

"You have to pay five dollars first."

Mrs Stonecutter clicks her tongue, as if it's a revelation to her that the point of a school fundraiser is to raise funds. She unzips the secret pocket in her leggings and hands me the money. I pass her the card and fill out the book. Baby Violet takes the card off her and starts drooling on it.

"I'll grab one of those too," Mrs Stonecutter says, pointing to the stack of *The Australian Women's Weekly Children's Birthday Cake Book – Vintage Edition* that Mrs Tagliatelle has set out for sale.

"That will be fifteen dollars, please."

"Fifteen!" exclaims Mrs Stonecutter. "I can get one for ten dollars at Big W!"

Mrs Stonecutter *really* doesn't understand the point of a fundraiser.

But she throws the money down on the table anyway and grabs a copy.

"Boys shouldn't be inside," are the last words she says as she heads out the door.

I don't believe her. But it still hurts me a little on the inside.

Mrs Tagliatelle always has her lunch twenty minutes after twelve. She puts the phone straight to voicemail and lets me follow her to the staffroom, where we sit down at the corner table. I always have a sandwich and Mrs Tagliatelle always has leftovers from last night's dinner. She brings in extra so that I can taste her home cooking.

Then she'll take out her phone and show me the latest photos of her dog, Golden Boy.

It's awkward sitting in the staffroom with all the other teachers, including Miss Babette and Principal Taylor, but no one questions my presence because of Mrs Tagliatelle. I heard Principal Taylor saying once that the whole school would fall apart if it weren't for Mrs Tagliatelle's organizational skills.

It's mostly awkward because of the time Roscoe found out where I went during lunch (instead of being outside kicking a ball around) and said wouldn't it be funny if I switched the contents of the sugar pot and the salt shaker in the staffroom kitchen around as a prank on the teachers. I said *no* and he went around telling everyone I was a wimp. That happened during the week before my birthday party last year. I wonder if it had anything to do with no one from school showing up to my party. Maybe Dad's computers can calculate the probability. Maybe not.

When the bell goes to signal the end of lunchtime, no one has come to claim the White Rabbit. Mrs Tagliatelle says the card can go in the bin.

"Mrs Stonecutter is right," she says. "The desiccated coconut does go everywhere."

I don't put the card in the bin though. Because I feel sorry for a rabbit that a) is not even a real rabbit, and is actually a cake and b) doesn't even exist because no one is going to bake it. I tuck the card into my pocket.

When I get home, I will put it in my secret shoebox. In it are random things like a rock and a shell and the empty wrapper of a chocolate Fantale. They aren't worth anything. The feather in it doesn't belong to a special exotic bird. But they all have a secret meaning to me.

I tell Dad about the theme of *Vehicles of the Future* for this year's Science Week and he seems impressed. We are sitting at the table tonight, eating the dinner Dad has cooked. He has bought sausages and pre-cut vegetables from the supermarket and baked it all in one pan. You could almost mistake it for a normal mealtime. Except Mum would cut up her own vegetables and also add crushed cloves of garlic and rosemary from the garden. But she's not here, sitting in her usual spot. Tears prickle in my eyes, but I try not to let them bother me.

Dad says that he envisions, in the future, vehicles hurtling through glass (or maybe high-resistance plastic) tubes in the sky. He says that when we start running out of room, we will stack things on top of each other, like homes and offices and parking lots. And that it's crazy we are still driving cars on two-dimensional roads where during peak times they can get jammed for hours. That wouldn't happen if roads were stacked on top of each other too.

Oh, and if cars flew.

I tell him that makes a lot of sense, but Miss Babette says we don't have to necessarily interpret vehicles as *cars*, and how Roscoe says he's going to invent one that runs on farts. As I tell this story, Dad starts to smile and says it's a brilliant idea to recycle waste. He drops his smile when he sees me frowning. Dinner doesn't taste great after that. I think it's because there's no rosemary in the potatoes.

Dad lets us have dessert afterwards – ice-cream with custard, jelly and fresh strawberries, which is different as well. Mum only let us have dessert on special occasions. She's always going on about refined sugars and saturated fats clogging our arteries. But Dad and I both feel better after eating it.

Dad then goes into his Man Cave and I follow.

After you flick the switch, the fluorescent tube on the ceiling takes ages to register. It blinks, like, a billion times and you can see Dad's sixteen computers in the dark, all blinking too, and it's like watching a really strange strobe show before the tube decides to come on for good. One of these days, I reckon it's going to blink one too many times and blow up.

Dad is very neat. The sixteen computers all sit on one side of the room and the brass section lives on the other, as if Dad is determined to keep both of his hobbies separate. I watch as Dad picks up the tuba and gives it a polish with his sleeve. Puts it back and then stares at it with a finger on his chin.

"How come you don't play them?" I ask.

"Hmm?" says Dad, as if he's lost in thought.

"Your instruments?"

"Shh," replies Dad. "I don't want to cause an argument with your mother."

I think Dad has forgotten that Mum doesn't live here any more.

I bet she's stretched diagonal on the hotel bed right now, watching a romantic comedy in a bathrobe and eating room service. But I don't remind Dad in case it makes him want to go back into the bedroom again and stare at the spot where Mum's bedside drawer used to be.

The ceiling in the Man Cave is made up of these funny felt-covered panels and one of them has fallen in. Dad says he will fix it on the weekend. He goes over to the other side of the room, turns on one of the monitors, and brings up an ancient computer game. It's one where a snake starts out as a dot and gets longer and longer, and you have to try to move it around the screen without running the snake into itself.

"Wanna have a go?" asks Dad.

I shake my head.

"You used to love it when you were a little tyke. Used to make you laugh and laugh."

"Well, I know better now," I reply, stroppy. "They make games with advanced graphics these days. Snake is lame. And it's not even a snake, it's a green line!"

I regret it as soon as the words come out of my mouth. Dad looks hurt. But I guess I'm still hurt from when he said Roscoe's fart car was a good idea.

Tiger slinks in and sits between us.

Dad shuts the game down and brings up a different screen.

"What are you doing tonight?" I ask Dad, trying to change the topic.

"I'm going to do a manual check to see if all my data is backed up," says Dad, sounding relieved we're talking about something else. "Sometimes you can't trust computers, even if they're set to automatic. They need a human touch."

We sit down in his high-backed swivel chairs that always make me feel like I'm in charge of a control centre. Dad puts his hand on the top of my head, like he does when he calls me his Little Man.

I smile.

"Why does that button on your computer say *Time Machine*?" I ask, pointing to the screen.

"That's what the backup software is called," answers Dad.

"Why *Time Machine*?"

"I guess because it can take me back to how the data looked at any point of time in the past," says Dad. "Like, for example, I can ask my computer to take me to this exact time last year."

Dad scrolls the bar backwards and clicks *we can go back*.

A whole bunch of folders pop up.

"One year ago, these were the experiments I was running on my computers. Remember the simulation of what would happen if the world suddenly stopped spinning and went in the opposite direction?"

I nod.

"This is an article I wrote on it for *The Curiosity Room* magazine...these were the songs I had on my playlist, 'Space Oddity' is the first one...and these were the photos I took that day."

Dad clicks on the photos folder.

That's when the photos from Reabold Hill pop up.

I thought Dad would immediately want to close them and go back to present time.

Instead, he makes the first photo bigger.

We look through the images of when the three of us hiked up Reabold Hill. The fourth photo starts to move, and I realize it's a video. In it, I can hear Dad's voice saying, "Well done! That's my Little Man!" and you can see part of my face smiling. The frame is mostly taken up by Mum doing a victory dance and shouting, "I told you! I told you!"

"Do you still remember that day?" asks Dad, as he continues scrolling through the photos.

"Yup," I reply.

"That last photo is my favourite," says Dad.

"Mine too," I say.

"Your mother's also."

We sit in silence for a while, looking at the last photo until it gets too sad. Then Dad closes everything down, and we leave it all in the past, one year ago.

"If it's possible for the computer to go back in time, then is it possible to build a real time machine?" I ask.

A new idea is whirring and forming in my head.

"Remember the space elevator simulation? That worked on the computer, but only hypothetically. As an idea," says Dad. "Anyway, I don't think a time machine is a good project for Science Week."

"Is it because you don't think it's a *Vehicle of the Future*? Remember how I told you that Miss Babette said not to get bogged down thinking that it means a car? A time machine does *travel*."

Dad shakes his head. "It's too complicated and has too many variables. Stick to something easier, champ."

The idea is still whirring and forming in my head, just in an angrier fashion.

A time machine is a way better idea than a fart car.

But I don't say anything to Dad.

THINGS THAT WILL NEVER HAPPEN AGAIN NOW THAT MY PARENTS ARE NOT TOGETHER

#3

Mum got the idea to hike up Reabold Hill because Mrs Stonecutter hiked it the week before and said there was a view at the top to die for. That it was an easy hill for beginners. "A cinch!" she put it.

If there was one thing that Mum thought we never did enough of, it was *family bonding time*. Dad pointed out the hill might not be "a cinch" to all of us. We'd never even hiked one hill before, whereas Mrs Stonecutter was the sort to run up and down Jacob's Ladder – which is made of two-hundred-and-forty-two steps and goes forty-one metres up one side of Mount Eliza – ten times in one go. And that would be before lunch.

Mum was determined about it, so one afternoon we set out with backpacks filled with water bottles, healthy snacks and sunscreen. Mum double-checked the weather forecast and it was going to be sunny all day with light southerly winds and zero per cent chance of rain.

I remember how the climb took longer than anticipated. The sun was looking like it was about to go down before we reached the top. I remember how my legs ached so badly it was almost like I couldn't feel them any more. I remember how heavy my backpack started to get; how it felt heavier even after I'd gulped down all the water and eaten all the sultanas and activated almonds.

But just as I was going to sit down in the dirt and never get up again...

We made it to the top.

I couldn't believe it.

I was convinced we'd be walking for ever.

And it *was* actually worth it.

Looking down at the city, it felt like we were on top of the world. I had this feeling inside, like I suddenly had a new perspective on life. Each of us felt proud of ourselves and also of each other. Dad put his hand on my head and said I was his Little Man. I forgot about my aching legs. Mum was buzzing around shouting, "I told you! I told you!" We were a team.

Mum made us all squish together in front of Dad's phone, because he has the longest arm, to take a selfie. All of us smiling. The perfect sunset in the background.

And that was how we took our favourite photo. Mum even had it printed and framed. It was the lock screen on both Mum's and Dad's phones for the longest time. Now Mum's has changed to a school portrait of me and Dad's is the Santa photo he made me take for a laugh.

I heard someone say once, or maybe they sang it in a song, that they wished they could live for ever inside a photograph. I think I understand that feeling now.

I want to ring Mum. I approach Dad so many times to use his mobile, but then I clam up and change my mind. He'd probably want to know what the matter is, and nothing is the matter. Not really. I don't want to worry Dad and I don't want to disturb Mum, since she's at the hotel and Mum loves hotels.

The House on the Hill doesn't have a bath, so the first thing she does on every holiday is to fill the hotel tub right up with bubbles. She'd spend hours in it, letting out the water when it starts to get cold and topping it up with hot water, making Dad look for another bathroom if he needs to go. She also likes to read in the bath and, every time, promises not to drop the book in. Right before she does.

I go to the study and stare at the books that belong to

Mum – the waterlogged ones that have expanded to twice their size, the pages refusing to stay closed any more. I wonder if she'll come back for them. Or if she'll decide they are best for the bin now that she's making a fresh start.

I need to get used to spending my Dad Days with Dad. And my Mum Days with Mum. Get used to making that distinction. And I should give *both* of their places names that aren't "home". *House on the Hill* and…*Flat on the Flats*?

I'll work on that one.

So, I almost ring Mum. But I don't.

I can't stop thinking about the Time Machine on Dad's computer. How it can take you to any point in time and show you what you were doing back then. What documents you were working on; what music you were listening to. What that day looked like if you had taken pictures. And how, if you had filmed a video, it's almost like looking down a wormhole back into the past.

In my head I can almost see how it'd work for time travel in real life. But some bits of it are unclear. I'm missing *something*, but as soon as I know what that *something* is, then it will make sense.

I think about Yan, who looks at the world differently to other people. If I get the nerve, I might be able to ask her what she knows about time.

I wake up the next morning earlier than Dad. By the time he's gone to the kitchen and set the coffee machine whirring, I've already changed into my school uniform, brushed my teeth, brushed my hair, packed my lunch and put my shoes on.

"No wearing shoes inside the house, kiddo," says Dad as he takes a sip of his black coffee and makes a face.

I thought that was Mum's rule because Mum is Chinese. When she first met Dad, she told me he'd happily wear shoes inside, and she had to train him out of it. I thought now that she didn't live here any more he would revert to his old life.

Guess some things take time to undo.

"Can I go to school now?"

Dad raises his eyebrows. "Go on, then. Remember, it's swap-over day. Mum will come here to pick you up after school. Maybe in time you'll just walk over to her place. We haven't quite worked out the finer details yet."

Dad takes another sip of his coffee and I head towards the front door. I notice that on the hallway table, the framed version of the family sunset photo is still there. Dad has not put it away yet. I guess there are a lot of finer details that need to be worked out in time.

*　*　*

I walk down the hill and find I'm being mirrored on the other side of the road. Yan is walking on the grass, her nose stuck in a different book this time. Something huge and bound in red leather. The sort of book I can already tell the smell of, even over here.

She walks into the same power pole that she did last time and stares up at it, as though she hasn't bumped into it before. In my mind, a picture of Yan bumping into the same pole, every single day of the school term, plays on repeat. Over and over.

I cup my hands to my mouth. "Yan!" I call out.

She stares up into the sky. Then straight in front of her. She finally turns to see me. She looks shocked, but I'm not sure what why.

"Come and walk on this side. Where there's a path!"

It's like I'd just suggested the wildest thing she's ever heard. She crosses the road and looks me in the face. Her eyes burn right through me.

Nestled in her arms is *Cambridge Babbage's Calculating Engines: Being a Collection of Papers relating to them; their History and Construction, 1889.*

I'm right. It does have that billion-year-old musty library pong.

"At least you won't bump into a power pole on this side," I say and swallow nervously.

"That's if the power pole actually exists," she says, as if she's correcting me.

"Why doesn't it?" I ask. I look across the road. It's still there.

I'm supposed to play it cool. Perhaps ask her about her book, and whether that means she's into science. Tell her that Dad is into science too. Ask what she thinks about the *Back to the Future* movies and if there is anyone else who considers the third movie their favourite. But instead –

"Do you think it's possible to build a time machine?" I blurt out.

She leans her head close to mine, as if she thinks someone might be listening in, even though there's no one around.

"Yes." Then, "Come and find me during lunch."

I'm not sure. Mrs Tagliatelle might get worried if I don't show up at the front office.

Yan does another strange thing before we reach the school. She picks up the black and white cat I sometimes see sitting on top of a brick letterbox and examines it carefully all over. Then she puts it back down. The cat licks the side of itself in indignation.

"Did you find what you're looking for?" I ask her, more as a joke than anything.

"One day I will," she replies.

In class we make a start on our Science Week projects. Despite what Miss Babette told us, almost everyone is making a poster on futuristic cars that look like ordinary cars but are flatter and sleeker and can fly or go underwater, and that no one can afford, unless the people of the future are all rich.

I don't care what anyone thinks. I'm making my poster about a time machine. It travels. It will exist one day. It's a *Vehicle of the Future*. I choose a piece of black card because I plan to draw the time machine in the middle and then have information boxes in white card. Once I figure out what the optimal time machine looks like. In the meantime, I start cutting out the letters T I M E in red card for my title.

Roscoe, who is sitting on the far left at a ninety-degree

angle to me, gives out a huge "Pfft!" which I'm sure is directed at me.

I don't bother looking up. Which is for the best anyway because after I finish cutting out my title, I start to get a bit sniffly, looking at it spell out TIME MACHINE.

Roscoe sees me, snorts and says loudly, "Boys don't cry!"

"I'm not crying," I reply softly, but more to myself.

I feel like I'm the only person in the whole class, the whole world, the whole universe who believes in my project. I shrink into my shell and become small. Insignificant. A speck in space.

But wait. Yan. She believes me. She told me to meet her at her spot. Everything expands a little bigger again.

I feel bad not going to find Mrs Tagliatelle during lunch. What if there's something important that needs checking today? An email or parent communication that's going to go out with a possible grammar error or an obvious spelling mistake? I also feel bad that no one's going to help her eat her double-sized lunch. But I'm sure Mrs Tagliatelle would understand that, if it wasn't for me needing to find the answer to a life-or-death situation, I wouldn't do that to her.

Yan hasn't told me where she goes during lunchtime. I've never seen her in the playground.

But I know exactly where she is.

I walk diagonally across the grassed quadrangle. A ball comes rolling at me and at that exact moment I know

I have two choices: to stop the ball with my foot, or to let it roll past me.

I decide to step to the side. I'm immediately greeted by groans from the group of kids coming towards me. Roscoe looks at me with his hands on his head like he can't believe it. But I know it's not stopping the ball that is the problem. It's being watched by this group of super sporty kids when I have to kick it back.

And I can't kick for crumbs.

This is what Dad calls a *Hobson's choice*, when something isn't a choice at all. It's not like I could have stopped the ball, booted it, had it shoot off at the right angle, bounce off the corner of the building, and then magically into the soccer net on the oval so the kids would carry me off on their shoulders like I was a champion of the world.

I asked Dad if Hobson's choice is mathematical and he said, "No, philosophical."

Then he went quiet, like he was thinking about something from his own life. He's not good at things that aren't mathematical. I thought he would say, "Go ask your mother," but he didn't.

Roscoe gives me a dirty look as he jogs past me.

"Why aren't you sucking up to the teachers today?" he spits out.

I ignore him and keep walking.

I'm right.

Yan is in the library. But I don't find her straight away. I guess, like a library book, I have to search for her.

The librarians – who are all huddled together at the borrowing desk with cups of tea and a tray of little sandwiches – don't tell me to leave. They give me a nod, a sort of secret look like I'm entering a special club. Then they turn back to their sandwiches.

I put my hands in my pockets, touch my sandwich there and walk past them like I'm here to find a book. I carefully check the first section of the library and try to predict if I can find her in certain sections. Maybe Cryptozoology, with books about giant squid and night-time mothmen and snow beasts with big feet, or Non-Fiction, where the computing and science books are.

She's in none of these places.

I find her tucked all the way up the back, on the floor of a section that is blocked off with a grey felt room divider and a laminated piece of paper that reads *Staff Only*.

"What the...?" I exclaim as I pass the sign.

It's like I'm stepping into a different world. There's a shelf of crusty textbooks from the nineties (and even earlier). A huge wooden drawer that used to house the index cards before there were computers to look up books. A spinning book stand that no longer spins. A pile of random old electronics, stationery and furniture.

Yan puts a finger to her lips. "If we keep quiet and don't make a fuss, they'll let us stay here for all of lunch."

She pats a spot on the carpet next to her. "This is where the library holds things it considers 'On the Way Out'," she tells me. She points at the shelf of textbooks and smiles. "I call that the Book Departure Lounge."

I take my sandwich out and sit down. Yan has a sandwich too and holds out one half to me. The filling is fried spam with a fried egg.

Sometimes, Mum will fry a slice of spam with an egg and I'll have it for dinner on top of white rice. So the fried spam and egg together is not new or weird to me. It's just that I've not seen them squished between two pieces of bread before.

Simultaneously, I feel a sense of familiarity and unfamiliarity.

Which doesn't make sense. Which shouldn't even be possible. But Dad ran an experiment on his computers once that proved that sometimes a particle can exist in two places at the same time.

Yan inspects the half of the sandwich I've offered her in return: margarine, honey and banana. Is she staring at it like it might be some clue to unlocking the secrets of the universe? But then I apply *Occam's razor*, which states that the simplest answer is often the best. That Yan hasn't seen this type of sandwich filling before. She takes a bite, shrugs and swallows.

"The library saved my life," says Yan. She eyes me warily. "I was at the monkey bars at the beginning of the school year, chatting with a bunch of kids and, before I knew it, the conversation turned. I must have said something *controversial*. Ma Ma is always saying I shouldn't be *controversial*, that there is something to be said for being submissive."

Yan waves her hand like she wants to flick that opinion away like a booger. "Anyway, they started chasing me. I don't know why I ran. If I didn't run, then they couldn't chase me, could they?"

She takes another bite of the sandwich.

"But I ran. Up ahead, I could see the library. Like a beacon. A sanctuary. It was almost shining. I slowed down and stepped in and found they could go no further. Like magic."

Yan puts her hand over her heart like a secret sign.

She suddenly reminds me of how Mum used to be at the end of the day. When she would come home from work and start cooking dinner even before she'd changed out of her work clothes. She had all these things stored up to tell me, like she had no one else to tell. And I'd always wonder why she didn't tell Dad.

"So, if it wasn't for this place, I wouldn't have anywhere to go."

Yan looks around at her safe space with thankfulness on her face. But at the same time with a sense of scepticism, as though she expects it all to be torn away and scrunched up like paper. Strangely, I feel like I understand her.

"Sometimes Ms Page, the head librarian, lets me help choose new books to order. She obviously thinks I'm a woman of taste."

"I came about the time machine," I blurt. "You say it's possible."

Oh no. I've put my foot in it. Again.

Yan, though, does not seem fazed. As if she had expected me to ask the question.

"The question is not whether time travel *is* possible," she replies, sitting up straight, "but more specifically – *why* do you want to go back in time?"

I don't want to tell her the truth. It's too personal. "For my Science Week project," I lie.

She shakes her head. "No. That's not a good enough reason. It needs to be for a very special, individual, distinctive, vital reason driven by the *Human Condition*."

I don't think I can tell her. I've only known her for three days. I wouldn't even think of telling my parents and I've known them my whole life. Plus, *they're my parents*.

And I don't know what the Human Condition is. I'll have to ask Mum about it. It sounds painful.

So instead I ask, "What makes you think you can build a time machine anyway?"

Yan answers like I should already know. "Because I've already done it."

I stare at her. She stares back at me. Unblinking.

"How far back are you hoping to go?" she finally says. "Please don't tell me 1955!"

"Um...maybe, like, a year back. Or so." I press my lips together, so I don't accidentally say anything more.

"Oh! That's fine," replies Yan. "Not a lot changes in a year."

That's not true.

Enormous shifts can happen within a year. Or in even less. If a meteor was heading towards earth, the length of time between seeing it in the sky and impact would only be five-and-a-half days. But I don't say anything in case she asks me any more personal questions.

The bell rings for the end of lunch. We both stand up and dust off the crumbs.

"If you can give me a good reason to show you my time machine, come and see me again tomorrow."

"Hey," I say quickly. "What's yours then?"

"My Human Condition? It's called *anemoia*."

I don't want to ask her what *anemoia* is, in case it's something private.

I guess that's another thing to add to my list to ask Mum.

Even though I don't have a proper reason relating to the Human Condition – don't even know what it means yet – I search for Yan again after school. But it's like the universe says *no*.

The library is closed. I know because I rattle the handle and it's locked. I can't see anyone inside, and the lights are off.

I watch for her on the way up the hill, expecting to see her mirroring me on the other side. No, hang on. I told her this morning that she should walk on the side where the path is. But she's not on this side either.

No big deal. I'll see her tomorrow.

Somehow, I still feel disappointed.

* * *

Neither of my parents have ever trusted me with the key to the house; they both think I'm going to lose it. So, the last adult to leave in the morning will hide it outside. If it's Dad, he keeps the key inside an industrial-strength box with a combination lock inside the gardening tub, under the decking of the house.

Mum always puts it under the doormat. Which is even worse than letting me have it because isn't that the first place a robber will look? They can walk right on in, over the cheerful doormat that exclaims *Welcome to the Greenaways!*

I won't have to look under the mat ever again. I let myself in, trying to think of something positive. *I guess the house will be...safer?*

The family sunset photo still sits on the hallway table.

Tiger comes barrelling down towards me so fast you can hear the floorboards creak. She wants a chin rub and gives me some big purrs. This is very uncharacteristic of Tiger as she's usually elusive and you have to go to her if you want something. Maybe it's because she's only getting the attention of two people now, instead of three.

I hate to break it to you, Tiger, but wait till the days you're stuck here with only Dad.

I give her an extra pat.

*   *   *

Tiger follows as I go into the kitchen and make myself a snack – a cheese toastie and two-minute noodles, chicken flavour. In the past, nobody really minded what I did before dinner. Usually, I would watch TV, or I'd talk to Tiger and hope she'd talk back. It's always been my favourite two hours because I get it all to myself, but today I feel agitated and can't enjoy it.

Now that Dad's in charge of the House on the Hill, he might insist I do my homework first thing. I'm hoping he'll keep things the same. After all, he was a computer and music geek when he was a kid and still is. Dad seems to prefer change when it's simulated on the computer and therefore only pretend.

Maybe it's Mum who'll change the rule at the Flat on the Flats. She has always hinted that the person she was ten years ago is not the same person she is today. She's definitely the sort to suddenly have a new idea one day – plant food trees to save the Carnaby cockatoos, or hike a different hill every weekend for the whole of summer – and just as suddenly it'll all blow away.

Now that they don't have to come to a compromise

with each other, they can do what they like.

What seemed safe and certain is now unpredictable and can't be known.

In my mind I see myself splitting, living two completely different lives depending on which half of the week it is. My stomach starts to do weird things, so I beeline to the Man Cave to try to find something that's comforting and will always be the same.

I'm actually glad to see that the panel on the ceiling is still in the process of sliding out. That's something that has been the same since for ever.

But sitting in the middle of the floor is a silver motorcycle. I've never seen it before. I've never heard Dad talk about motorcycles or seem remotely interested in them.

I close the door to the Man Cave and run back to my bedroom.

Back to where everything is the same and David Bowie is where he's always been, on the back of my door.

Mum comes at six o'clock to pick me up. My parents usually hug or give each other a peck on the cheek when they see each other for the first time after work, after a whole day of being apart. Mum explains it's their way of resetting and reconnecting. But today they stand across from each other and don't touch. They just look awkwardly at each other.

"How's everything?" Mum asks Dad, as though he's a stranger whose life she knows nothing about.

"I've dug Pop's old motorcycle out of storage. I'm thinking of restoring and riding it again," replies Dad.

I never knew Dad rode a motorcycle. He's never said anything about it. Ever.

I see a frown briefly cross Mum's face and then it's gone again.

She folds her arms stiffly in her suit jacket. He puts his hands in his trouser pockets.

Luckily, Tiger comes through the cat flap at that moment and starts going nuts, rolling around Mum's feet and trying to eat Mum's toes.

"She misses you," says Dad. It appears like he's going to say more. But he doesn't.

"You know I can't keep a pet at that tiny apartment, it would be cruel. Come here, boofhead," says Mum. She squats down and starts playing with Tiger.

I stand there awkwardly, with my school backpack over one shoulder and my overnight bag on the other, wondering what I'm supposed to do. Wait for instructions, I guess. I feel like my life is in a holding pattern.

"Let's go, James," Mum says. As she stands up, she stares sadly at Tiger.

I follow her down the hallway.

I watch as she turns her head to look at the sunset photo on the hallway table. For a moment I think she's going to reach her hand out to pick it up. Or to place it face down. But she doesn't do either and walks out the door instead.

* * *

It's been raining, so Mum's car smells like wet cats. I sit in the back seat because I want to be with my things, but I forget that that's where the smell is the strongest. After work, and sometimes on weekends, Mum helps to transfer cats between the Cat Haven and foster homes, between the Cat Hospital and foster homes, and between the foster homes themselves. When I was little, she convinced me wet cats smelt delicious, like carob, and when I pressed my nose against one of the shivering cats, I could almost imagine it had a chocolate centre.

Now that I'm older I know better.

"I've got you a new bed," says Mum, turning around in the driver's seat and smiling at me. "You'll really like it."

Something in my head tells me I'd rather have my broken trundle bed if things had only stayed the same.

"How was school?" she asks.

I think about Roscoe being mean and how he looked at me like I was an ant that he wanted to squash. About how I didn't go to see Mrs Tagliatelle at the front office and never got to explain myself to her. About Yan running away from a bunch of kids and then crossing a magical threshold into a safe space.

"It was fine," I reply.

Even if I wanted to tell her all these things, right now – in the back of a car that smells like a wet cat, travelling to a place I've only seen once and am now supposed to call home – does not feel like the right moment.

Maybe I would have said something if it had been another normal day. My parents both still together. Mum asking me the same question in my bedroom. David Bowie on the back of my door – with that look on his face that said he understood the whole universe – giving me the strength to tell the truth.

It takes us ages to get the front door open. Mum gives me a long list of excuses as we stand out there in the dingy hallway, the fluorescent light above us blinking and attracting moths. I'm terrified of moths.

"This is a really old door. I should get it looked at, but I don't know if I have the time to argue about it with the landlord. Wood warps in winter, so it might fix itself by summer."

After a bit of jiggling, the door miraculously opens, and Mum makes a grand gesture with her arms like she's a magician. Two elaborate armchairs with a patchwork pattern have appeared, along with a green rug that has an outstretched tiger printed on it. There is also a small flat-screen TV.

"Aren't they gorgeous?" Mum asks, plonking herself into one of the chairs. "Got them for a steal off Gumtree. You would not believe the wonderful second-hand things people are selling."

I decline to sit in the other armchair because it looks like the sort of thing that might be a disguised portal that makes you disappear off the face of the earth. I never knew Mum's taste was so...colourful?

"I tried to keep things...*neutral* when I was with your father," says Mum, as if she can read my face. "You know, beiges, creams and every shade of grey."

I've never seen Mum's face so disgusted before as it is with the idea of beiges and creams and greys.

Helga the house plant has found a home next to the balcony door. In the kitchenette, Mum shows me the mismatched and incredibly floral mugs and bowls she got from the charity shop. Basic things – like a new wooden spoon and a can opener that she reveals from the second drawer – seem to bring Mum great joy.

I nod to agree that the place does seem more like a home now.

In my bedroom, I find not the new bed Mum promised me, but a bright teal-coloured couch. She flits around nervously, as if waiting for my approval, but I don't know what to say.

"Oh, I forgot the magic! Otherwise it's just a couch – right?"

She pulls out the seat and the whole thing tumbles out in three sections and turns into a bed.

"Try it. It's made of memory foam. Like resting on a cloud."

I don't tell Mum that Dad would say that a cloud is made of condensation and if you tried to rest on one, you'd go right through and hurtle down to earth at terminal velocity. Not to mention that it would be cold and wet and extremely unpleasant. I try not to think of Dad at all.

I lie down next to Mum and I agree it's very comfortable. The most comfortable bed I've ever tried. She closes her eyes, like she's going to fall asleep right there. In Mum's room is an old spring mattress and I say we should swap. Even though I love my new couch bed and I don't really mean it. Mum says *no*, it's for me, and even though I feel selfish, I feel comforted on the inside.

So, I open up a little about my day.

"What does the *Human Condition* mean?" I ask.

"Why do you want to know?" Mum asks back. She doesn't sound suspicious, just curious.

"It's for a school thing," I say hastily.

"That's good!" Mum replies enthusiastically. "I know *Science Week* is very important and all that, but I'm glad to see the school focus on psychology."

Of course, Mum would say that. She's a psychology lecturer.

"So, what is it?"

"I guess," says Mum and then she lets out a breath, "it's about the things that we as humans all go through. Like life, death, love, loss, grief."

Mum pauses. "It's a *condition* because we're all very much inflicted by it. Every one of us. It doesn't matter what gender, ethnicity, age or religion you are. There is no escape from it."

Mum goes quiet and looks at her fingernails.

I notice that she is now wearing her wedding ring on her right hand.

I think about Yan and how she says my reason for

going back in time needs to be driven by the Human Condition. How Mum says loss is part of the Human Condition.

For dinner, Mum makes me my favourite, which is baked beans with two hash browns. I'm instantly suspicious because for starters this meal has *no vegetables*, even though in the past I've tried to argue that beans are a vegetable. Mum would always argue back and say only if they are proper beans like kidney or cannellini beans and I'd say, "Yuck, no thanks."

As I squirt tomato sauce on my hash browns, I watch Mum as she sits opposite me at the plastic trestle table and eats her two hash browns and a salad made from chickpeas, cucumber and goat's cheese, possibly the world record of worst things in one salad.

"Is this a trick?" I ask.

"What are you talking about?" she replies.

"How come you haven't made *that sort* of dinner like you normally make?"

"Oh!" Mum finishes chewing and puts her fork down. "It's just that after coming back from staying at the hotel and having my dinner cooked for me, I realised I want to take a break. I've been making dinners – usually two because you normally like something different than your father – for over a decade non-stop."

I'm not sure how to reply. Mum hated having to cook dinner? Why didn't she get Dad to do it more then? He made sausages and vegetables the other night so it's not like he can't cook. Maybe it was something more than that.

"What's *anemoia*?" I ask instead.

"You're asking a lot of complex questions today," Mum observes. She starts eating again. "This is a strange one. It's when someone feels wistful for another time and place, one that they've never known before."

I think of Yan, sitting beyond the *Staff Only* sign, among all the cast-off things from the library that are older than her. But seemingly at home.

"What about when you feel wistful for something you *used* to know?"

"That's plain old nostalgia," says Mum and smiles. She looks happy and sad at the same time.

* * *

I do my homework on the plastic trestle table and watch as Mum makes a practice rocket for the Summerlake Primary School Cake Competition. She's figured out how to use the oven with help from the neighbour in the apartment to the left. You have to press a clicker on the *outside* of the oven that ignites a flame. Luckily, she didn't go ahead and turn on the gas while sticking a BBQ lighter inside, as that could have caused what Dad calls a Mass Extinction Event.

Mum's cutting up the two cakes into the shapes the book says to, and it's making a bit of a mess. The cake is either too soft or the knife too blunt because it's mostly dissolving into crumbs. Mum stacks the pieces on top of each other and tries to secure it together with a bamboo skewer, which makes the cake fall apart even more. With a last-ditch effort in optimism, she lifts up what is left of the cake and positions it onto the cardboard fins.

It tips over onto its side and goes splat.

"I guess that's what you call a *failure to launch*!" says Mum.

It's actually called a *launch failure*.

But I laugh at her bad joke because Dad's not around to take one for the team.

THINGS THAT WILL NEVER HAPPEN AGAIN NOW THAT MY PARENTS ARE NOT TOGETHER

#4

This time last year, it rained non-stop for a whole week. Dad made a joke that we should get ready to build an ark. His jokes are no better than Mum's. But Mum laughed because someone has to take one for the team.

On the eighth day, the rain stopped. And the sun came out.

Dad sat on the damp sun lounger out the back and read the latest edition of *The Curiosity Room* magazine. I rode my push scooter round and round the clothes line and Mum went back and forth between the laundry and the clothes line with all the sheets, duvet covers and blankets she hadn't been able to wash while it was wet. It felt like summer had time-slipped into the middle of winter.

I found it fun to ride between all the flapping washing, trying to challenge myself not to have it touch any part of my body, making myself really dizzy in the process. Mum complained that my front wheel was going to catch on her laundry and drag it into the dirt. It seemed like she was more concerned about that than me tripping, even though she was the one who said I needed to go outside for fresh air in the first place.

All the laundry dried. And it was clean. Mum folded it into three washing baskets and left it by the couch in the living room. It was still there the next day when the rain started all over again. I was bored, sitting in front of the TV watching the same old kids shows. Before I knew it, I had brought chairs over from the dining table, joined them to the sofa and the coffee table and built a fort.

I knew Mum was going to bust me, but as I lay there on the carpet, looking up at the ceiling of my fort and listening to the rain, I felt calm and peaceful on the inside. I wasn't thinking of anything in particular, and that was a satisfying feeling.

To my surprise, the sheets parted and Dad popped his head through, followed by his whole body. He lay next to me on the carpet, staring upwards as well.

"What are you doing?" I asked.

"Hiding from your mum," he replied, and I couldn't tell if it was a joke or not, although his voice sounded pretty serious. I laughed anyway.

Even more surprising, Mum popped inside the fort from the other side and lay down next to me too. We stayed like that for a while, with no one talking.

Still to this day I have no idea what happened. If Dad really was trying to escape from Mum. If Mum really was trying to find Dad. Because when she did find him, she said and did nothing at all.

But it's a nice memory, the three of us staring up, listening to the rain. It smelt like fresh eucalyptus laundry powder and coffee. Whenever I feel like crying, I bring this memory up in my head. Which, these days, is all the time.

2 WEEKS 1 DAY 9 HOURS AND 0 MINUTES UNTIL GO LAUNCH

It's weird walking to school from Mum's place. We both leave at the same time in the morning, and she shows me the key before she slips it under her new doormat, which reads *Welcome if you have pizza or an Amazon delivery*. I find I don't worry about the key as much here, as I'm sure no one's going to bother to break in to steal two of the world's most outlandish armchairs.

It's weird to have to go in the elevator and watch as the numbers count down, as if towards some impending doom. But nothing happens except that the doors squeak open and I approach the school from a completely different angle. Mum says I'll get used to it.

It's actually quicker to get to school from Mum's apartment than from Dad's place. There's no hill to watch out on and it's all flat terrain, so I arrive early. Mum says it'll be a process of trial and error before I figure out how to get to school at the same time I normally do.

Yan is waiting at the gate. I pretend not to be excited because for some reason I had begun to get the idea that I would never see her again and that, eventually, everyone leaves. It's what Mum would call an *irrational fear*.

I see Yan's carrying a large colourful guidebook that has a clunky-looking retro computer and gaming cassettes as big as bricks on the cover.

"What's that?" I ask, pointing.

She lifts up *Program Catalogue for Your TRS-80 Colour Computer, 1980*. Shows me the first page that reads: *You're about to discover that your TRS-80 colour computer is... fun that never stops! Something for the whole family! An adventure just beginning!*

"Why do you bother reading that if you might never even find a TRS-80 Colour Computer in real life?" I ask.

Yan flips to a page with a retro rocket. *Play Project Nebula*, it says. *Four levels of play, ten levels of difficulty. Unlike any other space adventure!*

"Don't you ever dream?" she asks me, and her eyes go all hazy. "Don't you ever imagine, James?"

I think about a certain cake book that I have pored over every single birthday and made a Top Ten list in my head, hoping that *that year* would be *the year*.

"If only I had seven hundred and eighty-nine dollars I'd buy a TRS-80 on eBay to restore. One day," says Yan and gives the book a loving pat. "But right now, it's time."

On cue, Mrs Tagliatelle comes walking up and lets us in.

I don't really want to look Mrs Tagliatelle in the face in case she's disappointed about yesterday. But when I do glance up, I see her eyes dart over to Yan and then to me. No words pass between us, but she smiles like she understands. I feel better about the fact that she had to eat all her leftovers for lunch herself and that I might be seriously behind on the latest photos of Golden Boy.

Yan goes up to the library, knocks three times, looks through the windowpane and then waves. She lets herself in and I follow. The librarians are standing at the borrowing desk chatting and drinking tea. Yan waves casually to them and they wave back. She heads towards the back of the library and once again I follow her, past the sign that reads *Staff Only*, and we both step boldly into the space forgotten by time.

"So, have you got your reason for me?" says Yan as we sit down on wonky, broken office chairs. Mine only has four wheels. It's supposed to have five.

I'm embarrassed to tell her, so I sit there and swivel slightly to the left and then to the right. This causes another wheel to come loose and roll towards the pile of On the Way Out and then underneath it, probably never to be seen again.

"Okay," I spit out. I need to get it over and done with fast. "My Human Condition is...*plain old nostalgia.*"

Everything goes deadly quiet. I can hear the librarians chatting in the background, as if I suddenly have supersonic hearing.

"Shall we order a copy of this book? I've heard good things."

"No, I've heard it's written more for adults than children. Pass."

I expect Yan to laugh at me. I don't know why. Maybe because lately I've felt like the butt of a cosmic joke.

But Yan doesn't laugh. She looks at me like someone who wants to share a secret because she's kept it locked away for a long time. Someone looking for a friend to share a secret back. Because she's lonely, like me.

"I understand," she says. "Things aren't what they used to be like. And that is a very important affliction of the *Human Condition.*"

She points to a desk.

I wheel myself slowly forward as Yan does too. The seat tilts to the right but manages to hold my weight. Just. I reach my destination and don't dare move. I stare at the old computer that sits on the top. Bulky. Plasticky and. . .

Neon pink?

"Did you know computers used to come in flavours?" says Yan. "Blueberry, grape, tangerine, lime and of course *strawberry*. Which is what this one is."

Old technology is weird. Dad once showed me this strange rectangle that people would wear on their belts and use to communicate through beeps, like they were whales or dolphins.

"Are you ready?" Yan rubs her hands together and looks nervous.

I nod.

She slides a black box about the size of a portable radio between us. "Here it is," she says in a hushed tone.

I stare at it in silence. I must look confused.

"My time machine," she stresses.

Oh. I thought it would be…

Bigger.

Yan takes an ethernet cable, plugs it into the computer and connects it to the black box. It has a big dial on the front and a small digital display screen that reads:

00:000:00:00

I watch as she turns the dial backwards until the display screen reads:

24:000:00:00

"What I'm doing is setting the coordinates for twenty-four years ago. Now watch this. *James, are you watching?*"

1999. Neither of us were even close to being born yet. I have no idea what the world looked like back then. Surely it wouldn't be that different. It's not like dinosaurs were ruling the planet.

I wait to be taken back.

"See, what normally happens when you open up a webpage is that the server will automatically bring up the latest and most up-to-date version for you. Which is what normal people would want."

Yan makes a face at the last sentence, and fires up the internet on the computer.

"But this thing I've built –" she gives the black box an affectionate pat "– has a proxy inside. Did you know the word proxy comes from the late Middle English word for *procuracie* which means to appoint someone to act on your behalf? Anyway...watch this."

Yan confirms the coordinates.

Suddenly, the slick, modern page I'm looking at – which is mainly all white, with professional graphics and pleasant colours – turns into a garish bright purple thing. There is a background of stars that won't stop moving. Strange icons dance along the bottom. A pop song that I heard Mum play once and say it was her favourite back in high school blares out of the ancient tinny speakers. Yan quickly mutes the volume.

"What...is this?" I ask.

It honestly hurts my eyes. Like I need to put sunglasses on.

I'm hoping she'll get rid of the screen, but Yan stares as if she likes what she sees.

"This, my friend," she announces, "is how this same

website used to look back in *1999*. Sorry, I called you *friend*. A bit presumptuous, maybe."

"So, this is your...time machine?" I'm glad we're not facing each other so she can't see the disappointment on my face.

"Yes," replies Yan. "The proxy can request to retrieve the website at any point in time since the invention of the internet. As long as the data on the other end still exists."

I mean, the internet time machine is very cute and all...

It's just that I thought when she said *time machine*...

Never mind.

"I like the authentic experience of using a vintage computer and browsing the internet as it was back then." Yan sighs. I watch as she yearns for something she never even had.

Maybe it's similar to someone who dresses like they're from the Victorian era because they feel more comfortable in a bonnet and bustle, or someone who decides to shun modern society and become a Man of the Woods.

The bell rings then.

I trail behind Yan as she strides up to the librarians at

the borrowing desk and cranes her neck to look at the book list they're huddled around.

"Personally, I would order this one and that one," she says, pointing at the page. "And also, this. If you have the funds, of course. Boy, do I understand the difficulties that come from budgetary constraints!"

She turns back to face me. "I guess I'll see you again?" she says, unsure and hopeful.

I don't reply.

At lunchtime, I spend my time at the front office. Mrs Tagliatelle is pleased to see me, has plenty of leftovers to share, and there are new photos of Golden Boy, wearing sunglasses and holding two tennis balls in his mouth at the same time. I laugh, but not as loudly as I normally would.

I'm also not concentrating as hard as I usually would when Mrs Tagliatelle gets me to check an email announcement about the banning of a new toy that has gone viral in the playground, before she sends it to all the parents and guardians.

"You okay, pet?" asks Mrs Tagliatelle.

"Yes," I reply and pull my shoulders back. Try to stand up tall.

"It's okay if you're not," she says with a kind expression.

I really appreciate it, but I don't say so.

"There's a letter missing in *school* here," I say. "It's spelt as *shool*."

"Thanks, pet," replies Mrs Tagliatelle.

2 WEEKS 0 DAYS
20 HOURS 13 MINUTES
UNTIL GO LAUNCH

Mum is at a loss. She wants to have a bath, but the apartment doesn't have one, only a small and slightly mouldy shower cubicle with pipes that scream at you if you don't turn the hot water tap fast enough. She shows me a foldable, portable plastic bath on the internet and we both frown over it.

A while later, as I'm trying to do my homework, I hear the banging of tins. The oven clicks on. Mum's making another trial cake for the Summerlake Primary School Cake Competition.

This time, she leaves the cake longer in the oven so it firms up a little more, and she lets it cool down completely before she starts hacking it up. She manages to make the body of the rocket and balance it on the cardboard boosters. It just has one chopstick in the middle that Mum is too scared to take out. She says it might be the only thing holding it together.

Carefully, she cuts out a final set of boosters and starts covering them with tinfoil, working on the breakfast bar because there's not enough bench space inside the kitchenette. I sit on the opposite side, flicking through *The Women's Weekly Children's Birthday Cake Book*. It really is my favourite book in the world, and I can never get enough of looking at the Paint Box or the Log Cabin or the Guitar.

All of a sudden, I want to tell Mum that I've secretly kept a Top Ten list in my head for every birthday. I want to tell Mum that I don't care if her cake is not perfect because I'd love it anyway. I want to tell Mum that I don't know why she never made me a birthday cake from the book, even though every year she says she will, but it doesn't matter any more.

"What's the matter?" says Mum, looking up. "You've been very quiet."

The words evaporate and all that comes out of my mouth is a mumble. "It's a question for Dad."

Mum smooths a piece of foil against the cardboard.

"I'm sorry you only get to see your father half the time

now," she says quietly. "I don't want you to think you have to halve the questions you normally have."

All the words suddenly come back, a tidal wave at the back of my throat. But nothing comes out.

"Maybe I can try to answer your question?" Mum continues, her voice still soft. "It was nice when we...had that little philosophical chat yesterday. I mean, if it's got to do with science then I'll probably get it wrong. But if I don't know I'll be honest and say I don't know."

I look at Mum, her face so hopeful.

"What is it called," I say slowly, "when you have variable x and you expect outcome y...but instead you end up with...outcome z?"

Mum's face, scrunched up in concentration, is suddenly filled with relief.

"Oh! I thought it was going to be about what would happen if everything on earth suddenly lost gravity for precisely five seconds. I can answer this question!"

Mum puts down the completed booster section and picks up the second one.

"It's like a dramatic turn of events in a play that the main character, and the audience as well, is not expecting. It's what the French call a *coup de théâtre* or a—"

"*Plot twist*," I finish for her.

"Precisely. A *plot twist*! Why do you ask, treasure?"

"I couldn't help being disappointed today when..." I think about the black box with the big dial on the front and the small digital screen. "Something didn't turn out to be what I thought."

"But are you okay about it?"

I think about how the time machine was really just an internet time machine. But it's not Yan's fault. She's clever to invent an internet time machine. I could never make anything like that.

"I'm okay," I reply.

"I understand that you're going through some big changes," says Mum gently, as if she knows what I'm really talking about.

We both look at the stray piece of foil that flutters from her hand, as it spins round and round before it lands on the floor.

"Does that answer your question?" says Mum, sounding sheepish. "I'm sorry that—"

"No...that was great, Mum. Thank you."

She looks back at me with tears in her eyes. Oh no. I hope Mum doesn't embarrass me by crying. Not that anyone is around, but you know.

"My answers might not always be the best, or the ones you want to hear, but I'll always try."

I get the weirdest feeling then. Like I've fallen into a different dimension, because in the one I left behind, I would have gone straight to Dad to ask the question instead of Mum.

But Mum gave me a good answer, she really did. Suddenly I get another weird feeling, like I'm seeing her in a different light. Like I'm seeing her as a whole person instead of just the *Mum* that is *Mum and Dad.*

"Drats," says Mum. She's covered the cardboard sections of the boosters perfectly with tinfoil, but when she goes to insert them together, the foil crinkles and tears.

"Do you have to cover them in foil?" I ask.

"Even though it's not a real rocket, James," says Mum, "it helps with the illusion."

The Undecided Days arrive. The Saturday and the Sunday that Mum and Dad haven't worked out what to do with, because a week isn't an even number. I wake up in my super comfortable new bed and I'm almost tempted to stay the weekend because of it. Mum is out on the balcony, her dressing gown blowing in the wind like a white flag.

"I want to keep him here," she says into the phone as she paces back and forth. "I'm thinking about renting two electric scooters and riding up and down the coast where the scenic bits are. He would love that!"

Mum pauses and listens for ages. Seems like Dad has his own ideas.

I go to put two slices of bread in the new toaster.

"James!" Mum comes stomping back in through the

glass sliding doors. "You can stay here today and go electric scooter riding – or go back to Dad's and help him restore Pop's motorbike. It's your decision!"

Mum stares at me like she expects me to make the correct choice.

"Um." I pause. "I'll go back to Dad's."

I'm only saying this because I hardly have anything at the apartment. All my *stuff*, including every item of clothing I own, is back at the House on the Hill. Here I only have an overnight bag. I don't feel at home; I feel like I'm at a sleepover.

I want to tell Mum it's not personal. That if Dad had been the one to move out and she had stayed at the old house, I would have chosen to spend Saturday with her.

Mum doesn't get it. Or maybe she does, but it still hurts. I see her tuck her feelings behind a smile for me, as she lets Dad know he can pick me up in an hour. She hangs up, drops her shoulders, and then comes into the kitchenette to make two mugs of milky tea.

"Let's go sit outside on the balcony. Enjoy the view."

It's freezing cold out there. Mum is wearing her flannel pyjamas, a woollen cardigan and her dressing gown on top of that. I've only got my pyjamas 'cos I didn't think to bring anything else. The steam rises off our mugs like a fog machine.

"I'll get proper chairs soon," says Mum.

We're sitting on two milk crates.

"It'll be more of a home then," she adds, and it comes out sounding like an apology.

Dad stands in the little space that is not really a hallway, and doesn't come any further in. He doesn't ask for a tour and Mum doesn't offer.

"Ring me around dinner time," she instructs and straightens my collar like I'm a little kid. Once again, I stand awkwardly with my school backpack over one arm and my overnight bag over the other.

My parents don't say goodbye to each other. It's only once I'm in the lift that I realize they didn't even say hello to each other. Should I even use the word "parents" any more? That word sounds like it should be used for a set of two people who are together.

"Where did you park?" I ask Dad. Mum says they are quite strict about visitors only parking in the bays that are marked with the word *visitors*.

"I didn't park anywhere," replies Dad. "I walked here."

"Why did you do that? I could have walked back to the house myself," I grumble.

Dad attempts to take my overnight bag off me, but I won't let him. He acts like he's upset the day has already started out wrong. I know Dad well enough to know when he's nervous about making the wrong impression. I've seen him make that same face when he was doing practice questions for an interview about extinction events with *The Curiosity Room* magazine and couldn't get his answers right.

I don't know why today has turned into such a big deal. You'd think it was the last Saturday left on earth.

We walk in silence, which I prefer.

Dad tries looking at me, but I don't look back at him. So instead he looks at the sky, at the footpath and then at a glittery handmade cardboard sign that reads:

Garage Sale 9am to 3pm.
Everything must go!

"C'mon, let's go and see. I promise I'll buy you one thing."

"Anything?" I ask.

Dad knows he's getting himself into trouble. "All right," he says, and we follow the arrow.

We're the first to arrive. The man has just finished setting up the tables in the garage and is affixing the last of the price stickers.

"Good morning," he says. "Feel free to make an offer on anything. We're moving house next weekend!"

I walk past the plastic toddler toys and Playdoh playsets until I reach the Lego. The sets are all individually bagged up with instruction booklets and everything. I pick one up that's a space shuttle. I look over to Dad. He's holding up a space helmet.

No. Not a space helmet. A motorcycle helmet, silver coloured, with a plastic face shield.

I put the bag of Lego down and go over.

"What do you think, champ?" he says and places it over my head. "You'll need one of these once I get Pop's motorcycle going."

I'm a spaceman, floating in a stranger's garage full of space junk.

I take the helmet off and pass it back to Dad. I'd definitely choose that over the Lego. The Lego set is cool, but the helmet is a lot cooler.

That is, until I go over to the kitchen section and I see among the brand-new novelty appliances – the doughnut maker, slushie station and candyfloss machine – a whole bunch of cake tins. I go over and sort through the shapes and pick up two round tins the same size.

"Does this count as *one thing*?" I ask Dad, holding both up.

"I guess so," replies Dad, confused.

"Then I want to get these."

"What about the helmet?" says Dad.

"I'd prefer these instead," I say, and I pass the tins over to the owner of the garage.

"It's good that boys can have any sort of hobby these days," the man says to me in a jovial voice. He hands me the tins in a brown paper grocery bag.

Dad scowls at the helmet in his hands. "Well, I'm going to buy this for myself!"

It's quite embarrassing to walk down the street when you're trying to behave normally, and your dad has a motorcycle helmet on his head.

When we get back to the house, Tiger comes running

down the hallway and jumps so high up against my body that her front paws touch my chest. She has never done anything like this before. When I used to come home from a whole day at school, she'd glare at me and then go back to cleaning herself, as if me just looking her way had soiled her fur.

I think about how in the past Dad would get so absorbed in his experiments that he'd forget to feed Tiger and how Mum would always get mad. I go to her food station. There's half a bowl of biscuits and the water is topped up.

Tiger follows me to my bedroom as I put my things down. Watches as I open my secret shoebox and take the White Rabbit card out. I slip it into the brown grocery bag with the cake tins and leave it next to my schoolbag, so I'll remember for Monday. I go to find Dad in the Man Cave and Tiger follows me there too.

The ceiling panel that was falling down has been pushed back into place. But another panel on the other side of the room is now easing its way out. Dad is on the floor, crouched over the drop sheet where he's laid out all his tools. I pick up the old motorcycle helmet that used to belong to Pop – black with a yellow, orange and red trim – and put it on my head.

"Hey! That's my helmet! You use the one from the garage sale!"

"You said you bought that one for yourself."

I sit down in the sidecar of the motorcycle. Tiger jumps in with me.

"Do you think we can make a helmet for Tiger?" I ask.

"There's an old polystyrene ball lying around that you can experiment with," replies Dad. "I might have this thing running before dinner, champ."

Dad does not have the motorcycle running before dinner. He still hasn't got it running by Sunday evening. Mum is grumpy when I talk to her on the phone because I've stayed inside most of the weekend.

"We could have gone electric scootering together and got lots of fresh air," she says to me.

Mum is obsessed with the amount of fresh air I get, like I should be on a quota. But I'm sure she'd still be grumpy if the motorcycle had been up and running, because she thinks it's dangerous.

To be honest, I haven't minded this weekend at all. I found the polystyrene ball Dad was talking about and started hollowing it out into a helmet for Tiger. She doesn't like it when I try to take measurements of her head with Dad's measuring tools. I'm going to spray the helmet with silver paint once it's finished so it'll look really flashy.

After a pizza dinner, where Dad burns the edge of the crust black, Deconstructed Dessert is served. It's exactly what it sounds like. Dad is allowed to buy whatever unhealthy sweet junk he likes now Mum is not around, so he's gone over the top. The pantry and fridge look like they've been stocked by, well...a kid like me. He takes what is expiring first, smashes it together and makes a dessert out of it.

We sit on the couch, each with a warm mug filled with ginger cake, apple pie, caramel, custard and whipped cream. Dad is so happy he's regressed back to his glory days. He plays his favourite album from the nineties and it's me who's sitting there quite sensibly, while he succumbs to the sugar rush and is literally bouncing off the walls, doing air guitar and drums.

But at the same time, I can tell Dad is really sad on the inside. After a while he goes quiet and puts on his favourite movie from when he was a kid. We've only seen it together once and it was a big deal. He told me we'd only ever watch it again if he felt like he needed to go back to a time when he had no problems and nothing to worry about.

Being a kid myself, I can honestly tell Dad that I have plenty of problems and lots to worry about. It's been so long he's probably forgotten what it's like to be one.

I let Dad curl up under the duvet he's brought out from the bedroom. He looks so lost I almost give him a pat on the head like I'm the adult.

But I don't.

The movie is about a bunch of kids who are hackers, and this computer program they find in cyberspace that plays games with them like chess, checkers and backgammon. Except the computer program can't tell what's a game and what's not and plans to launch nuclear weapons.

In the end the kids get it to play noughts-and-crosses against itself. The computer learns that each game ends in a no-win situation and that it's the same with launching the nuclear weapons. That the winning move is *not to play at all*.

I don't like the movie as much as Dad does, but I don't have the heart to tell him. Dad cries at the ending and I don't say anything because I'm certain now, despite what

Roscoe Stonecutter says, that it's okay for guys to cry.

"Is the winning move really not to play at all?" I ask Dad.

Dad goes quiet for a bit. "Sometimes we are forced to make a choice. If it's wrong, then that's life," he says. "Because we're humans, not computers."

I have to really consider this answer.

But before I can think too deeply, Dad says, "C'mon, James. Let's have a second round of Deconstructed Dessert."

THINGS THAT WILL NEVER HAPPEN AGAIN NOW THAT MY PARENTS ARE NOT TOGETHER

#5

The best day of Dad's life arrived in time for his birthday last year. Although he did hastily correct himself to say that the best days of his life were actually when he married Mum and when I was born, both being a tie.

This was when Dad first found out that our local independent movie theatre was going to play his favourite movie and he would have the opportunity to show me on the big screen. At the cinema proper, with popcorn and "the trimmings", the way he saw it when he was a kid and it changed his life.

The movie was playing in the evening on a Wednesday. Dad wanted to take the day off, but there was an important meeting he had to have in the morning at the CSIRO, so the best compromise was being allowed to leave work early. I remember waiting in the foyer of the cinema with Dad, trying not to eat the delicious-smelling jumbo popcorn in my hand and resisting the temptation to rip open the packet of chocolate Fantales.

Dad kept checking his watch. The previews were about to come on and Mum still hadn't arrived. My popcorn was going cold, the ice in my large drink was beginning to melt and I kept dropping the Fantales. The first movie preview started playing; we could hear it coming out from the cinema, even though we were still standing in the foyer. Then the second preview played.

Mum arrived. Finally.

The three of us sat down just as the last preview finished and the lights dimmed. I felt so relieved.

The movie didn't quite live up to the expectations Dad had built up in my mind. It was old and didn't have the grand special effects and things modern movies have.

It was *okay*.

When Dad asked me what I thought, I said it was the best.

What *was* great was that Mum actually seemed to enjoy this movie, even though she hates movies in general because she says they are filled with awful messages –

and she's talking about the G-rated ones. She laughed at the jokes and got genuinely worried for the characters, and I thought she was going to shout at the computer when it wanted to blow up the world. In fact, we all laughed at the jokes and were genuinely worried for the world in the movie.

At one point we all reached for the popcorn at the same time and bumped hands and we giggled in the dark.

This is the only memory I have of the three of us going to the movies together. Now there's no chance of it ever happening again, even if one day they make the big-screen version of my favourite book.

1 WEEK 4 DAYS
9 HOURS 59 MINUTES
UNTIL GO LAUNCH

For once I'm excited to go to school on a Monday.

Because I'm excited about the cake tins.

I tell Dad as he's warming up his coffee machine that I'm going to leave early for school again today. Dad gives me a puzzled look but doesn't say anything. He takes a sip out of his mug that reads *I make horrible science puns but only periodically.* I've heard that adults can't think properly before their first coffee of the day.

I'm walking down our garden path, craning my neck to spot Yan. But she's not there on the other side. Surely, she would leave for school at exactly the same time each day. According to my calculations she should be parallel to me right this instant...

A hand taps me on the shoulder, and I yelp.

"Sorry about that," says Yan from halfway inside a bush.

"What are you doing on this side of the road?" I ask.

"Just a reconfiguration," Yan replies. "Knowing how things are going to end. If I walked on the other side, you'd call me over anyway, like you did last time. It's predictive analytics."

I'm bamboozled, but she's...

Right.

"I've got a present for you," I say. I hold out the brown grocery bag.

She stuffs *Practical Interfacing Projects with Commodore Computers, 1985* into her backpack, takes the bag and peers inside.

"The White Rabbit is still up for grabs," I say. "I was thinking if your mum had the right tins, then she could make the cake."

I want to tell her that it's the first year my mum is entering the contest too.

Yan looks up and give me a smile. But it's a funny one, all crumbly.

"James, I wish it was about the cake tins," Yan says. "But my mum is Chinese. She won't participate in the competition."

"So what? My mum is Chinese too," I say.

I'm not sure why I say this with uncertainty. Mum definitely looks Chinese. Although her hair is not black. She dyes it, and she says it's because of her grey hairs, but I don't get why she chooses a colour called *medium ash brown*.

"Your mum was born here, right?" says Yan. "Well, my family only moved here five years ago. We still don't properly belong, in a way."

I guess Mum's not very Chinese after all. She fits right in with all the other Western academics at the university and has been known to use English words even they haven't heard of. My grandparents are *very Chinese*, and I once heard them use a term around her, *fen kai*. I looked it up in Mum's English-Mandarin dictionary and it translates as *separate*.

I don't know much about Ah Ma and Ah Gong, as Mum makes me call them. We only see them on the other side of a restaurant table at Lunar New Year, when Mum spends the whole time uncharacteristically saying nothing and staring down at the ends of her chopsticks.

"But the cake baking competition is open to everyone," I say.

Yan doesn't reply to this. We both keep walking down the hill.

She takes another peek inside the paper bag.

Maybe Yan's mother won't enter the contest. Maybe when Yan grows up and if she decides to have kids *she* will. But the future seems so far away. Who knows if this school will even run the cake contest then? Who knows if those cake tins will be around? Maybe they will disappear and one day show up at another garage sale.

"I'm really grateful for your present though. I could see on your face how excited you were. That's a very Chinese thing – more of an honour to give than to take."

I wonder who I really am.

We reach the gate and, after two minutes, Mrs Tagliatelle lets us in. We head straight for the library, knock three times and let ourselves in. The librarians are gathered with their cups of tea around a subscription box that they are slicing open with a pair of scissors. Yan gets distracted and goes to join in. I watch as they take out each book individually and pause to *ooh* and *ahh* at it.

"Sorry," says Yan when she comes back. "That was too exciting to miss out on."

"You don't have to keep apologizing for stuff," I tell her.

"Maybe I want to," replies Yan. "I come from a family that never says *sorry* or *I love you* or *putting that through the washing machine wasn't a good idea but that's my fault.* I'm making a version of myself that I want to be. The *Future Me*. Not the same old, same old my parents are."

I think about Yan in the future and I can see very clearly the person she's going to become. Confident and self-assured, speaking through a little microphone at her mouth to a large auditorium of people wanting to learn how to live up to their true potential. When I think about myself, all I see is a dotted outline around a white space, with a question mark in the middle.

At the back of the library, we pass the Staff Only sign. Once again, I look at the big pile of On the Way Out. Then I look at the home that Yan has made for herself, all the discarded items she's carefully recovered and set up and fixed. How she's made a cosy nest, like a mouse.

Yan puts back *Practical Interfacing Projects with Commodore Computers, 1985* and picks up *Mathematica: A System for Doing Mathematics by Computer, Second Edition, 1991.*

"I know the librarians have been meaning to chuck these for ages," says Yan. "But no one wants to because to do it properly, you have to rip the cover off and then put both bits in the bin. Nobody wants to kill a book. Even though it's not alive."

Yan invites me to sit down on the wobbly office chair and I do.

The *plot twist* being that I actually do want to be there. Even if Yan has no time machine.

I try not to move, as I don't believe the chair can afford to lose another wheel.

"I was thinking about yesterday," says Yan. "Sorry, do you even want to talk about it?"

I nod. I know I've only been here twice, but it already feels like a safe space.

"When you say you want to go back," continues Yan, "what do you mean by that exactly?"

I take a deep breath. "Does it make sense when I say I want to live inside a memory?"

Not that I've settled on one particular memory. I have a few good contenders, but thinking about it hurts my head and, even more, my heart, so I can only do it in little bits.

"I often wish I could live inside a photo," says Yan, completely unexpectedly. "Like when I see one of a field of sunflowers, or a scene of a quaint cottage with the lights on inside and a curl of smoke coming out of the chimney."

"Just for the rest of time to stop," I say.

"Just to be in that feeling," says Yan.

"I don't want to go back and for time to move forward again to the present day. I want to go back to that one moment when everything was perfect, when I was happy, like *really* happy, and stay there for ever."

We both sigh at the same time.

Embarrassed, we take a big breath. Also at the same time.

"Suppose we talk about it some more, outside of school," says Yan, slowly exhaling. "I've always hoped for the day I'd be able to go to someone's house...as a friend."

Yan shuffles nervously in her seat. It's a miracle no wheels fall off. "So, what are you doing after school today?" she asks.

"Nothing," I reply and smile.

In class, Miss Babette says we should go around in a circle and take turns telling everyone what our Science Week poster is about. Roscoe talks arrogantly about his flatulence car.

The seats have rotated and unfortunately he's next to me again, this time on the right. The class snigger and stare at him like he's a rock star while he repeats the word *flatulence* loudly in front of our teacher. It's highly juvenile and I do not participate.

When it's my turn I do my best to explain my time machine.

"It travels like a vehicle does, forwards and backwards. But in *time* instead of on terrain. I believe in the future it will be a common and real science."

"How does your time machine work?" Roscoe whispers to me. "Is it powered by an iced sponge, Cake Committee Boy?"

I'm proud that I've been around these past two years to assist Mrs Tagliatelle when no one else has ever bothered to ask if she needed help. And how does he know about my badge, anyway? I've made sure it's always hidden under my fleece jacket. Not that I'm ashamed of it or anything...

"Shut your stupid mouth," I say to Roscoe.

I'd forgotten to whisper back.

I'd also forgotten that even though Roscoe had said *flatulence* a billion times this morning already, Miss Babette considered *stupid* a swear word.

"Apologize to Roscoe right now," says Miss Babette.

"No!" *I hate Roscoe.*

"James! Apologize to Roscoe or I'll send you to the principal's office!"

The thing is, I'm tired of being treated as a joke. *Can't kick a ball properly. Can't come up with a proper Science Week project. Can't get anyone except my two cousins to come to my birthday party.*

And Miss Babette didn't even ask what he said to me first.

I won't apologize.

I end up at the principal's office.

I sit awkwardly in the chair opposite Principal Taylor.

Principal Taylor has been the head of this school for so long he was around when Mum was a kid.

"He's changed though," Mum had told me once. "Hang on, let me rephrase that. He's still exactly the same. He just no longer gives the cane."

"What is the cane?" I'd asked.

"When you were naughty, you used to get sent to the principal and he would whack you on the palm with a special stick," replied Mum in a low voice. "I remember this one boy, Jamie, he got caned a lot. I felt so sad for him."

"Did you name me after Jamie?" I'd asked and Mum went quiet.

I'm not sure I liked the idea of being named after a naughty kid. But if it's true...should I be touched that Mum named me out of compassion?

I keep my hands deep in my pockets even though Principal Taylor doesn't have the cane any more. I wonder when they ended the cane and if he secretly kept it. That's a scary thought. But not as scary as the fact that there must have been a special school supply shop selling canes.

"You'll have to write a letter of apology to young Mr Stonecutter." Principal Taylor stares at me over the top of his glasses. "Outlining your remorse. We don't raise bullies at this school."

That part hasn't changed. Mum told me that Jamie had to write a letter describing how the cane felt and then read it out to the whole class. She said that before school the next day, a few of the kids in the class – made confident by being in a group – had started hassling him. Mum said the group had called out to her and asked her to join them. Mum had turned away.

I said she did the right thing, but she replied, *Did I?*

Mum said turning away wasn't good enough. She wished she could turn back time. She wished she could have taken him by the hand, and they could have *run away*. She wished she could tell him *sorry*. I don't know why she tells me stuff like this, stuff she never tells Dad. I don't know why I choose to remember. She said she's tried looking for Jamie online over the years and she found plenty of people with the correct first and last name, but it's the face that is never right.

I put my hands back into my pockets at home time, my head down, hoping to avoid any sort of confrontation. The gate is right in front of me. It's open and I hope to sail on through.

Except, beyond the gate, I see Mum's car.

I don't know why she's parked in the ten-minute parking zone. It's not even my day to go to Mum's. In case she's forgotten, her days are Wednesday to Friday (and every second weekend, as it's now been decided).

But before I can get annoyed about it, Roscoe is in my face.

"Go away," I tell him. "I'll apologise to you in front of the class tomorrow."

"You're a loser who has no friends!" he yells at me.

"I thought *you're* supposed to be my friend," I say. "Remember? Your mum is best friends with my mum, and if she finds out we're not friends you'd probably get into trouble."

Roscoe looks taken aback by my answer. His face goes

all red. "Well, *not counting me*...you have no friends!"

"Yes, he does. I'm his friend," says Yan, sliding into the conversation.

She pulls my fleece jacket and drags me determinedly away.

"What was that about?" I hiss at her.

"Keep walking," she says. "This isn't a story where you become a hero and punch the bully in the face."

"The winning move is *not to play at all*," I reply and surprise myself.

"That's correct," says Yan, equally as surprised.

We pass through the school gates, right down the middle, with the other kids running around us. But it's like we're walking too fast. Or they're moving in slow motion.

"How come I've never seen you after school before? Well...until just then."

Yan doesn't answer. Instead she says: "You know how we discussed this morning about me coming over to your place? Is that...still on?"

I nod.

Mum gets out of the car and smiles down at Yan, but not at me. She has that sad-tender look on her face, like when she sees birds kept in too-small cages or puppies being advertised for sale on Gumtree.

The next car in line to take the spot honks. The driver holds up his wrist to point to his watch.

"Why are you even here?" I ask Mum.

She doesn't answer. I guess it's bad so she's going to leave it till later.

"Can I please have Yan over?" I try asking instead.

"We'd be delighted to have a visitor!" Mum says brightly to Yan, still ignoring me.

The two of us get in the back seat. Mum takes her sweet time sliding into the driver's side.

"Do your parents know where you are?" Mum asks Yan.

"No, Aunty," replies Yan, putting on her seat belt.

Mum asks for her home phone number and rings it as we drive off.

"Hello?" says Mum in her normal Western Voice. The speakerphone voice on the other end replies in English that she doesn't speak English.

That's when Mum puts on her Chinese Voice. I've seen her do this at the Asian Mart and Chan's Seafood Emporium. It's not just about Mum switching to a different language. As soon as her accent changes, the way she talks changes. She becomes serious, unsmiling, and her voice drops a few octaves lower.

When she speaks English, Mum is no-nonsense, confident, opinionated. When she speaks Chinese, she becomes...

Docile. Meek. Quiet. It's like she changes into a completely different person.

I try to listen in, but my Chinese isn't very good. Mum says I need more practice, but she won't force me to go to Sunday Chinese school and I don't want to go anyway. How will I fit in at a Chinese school when I'm only half Chinese? I don't even fit in at my school.

The woman on the other end of the phone doesn't seem very convinced by the idea of Yan going to someone else's house, but seems convinced by Mum's Chinese Voice. Mum hangs up. Returning to her normal self, she says to me: "How on earth did you end up at the principal's office? Didn't I teach you better and haven't you listened to any of my stories about Principal Taylor?"

Oh. So that's why Mum came to pick me up.

"Roscoe said my Science Week vehicle is made of cake!" I reply.

"Why didn't you clap back and say his Science Week vehicle is made of farts?" Yan interjects.

"His Science Week vehicle *is* made of farts!"

"Oh," says Yan with a solemness to her voice.

That's when I laugh.

Mum starts laughing because she's one of those people who laughs at other people's laughs. Then Yan is laughing too. I'm not sure why, but if I asked, she'd say she was laughing at the absurdity of the universe. Or something like that.

"Okay, just because we're laughing doesn't mean you can be a bully," says Mum after she calms down. She eases the car into the communal driveway, and raises the clicker to open the creaky green gate.

"And before you say you're not the bully, know that no one considers themselves a bully when they're the main character in their own story. If this story was from Roscoe's point of view, then you'd understand why he does the things he does. Think about it."

"I'm thinking about it," I grumble and get out of the car. "Sorry, Mum, for making you drive to school to pick me up."

Yan stands in the pothole-filled parking lot and stares

up at the apartment block. Stands very still. Doesn't stop staring.

"I wanted to make sure you were okay." Mum comes over and puts her hand on my shoulder.

"Yeah. I'm okay. Don't worry about it," I mumble.

But as I'm about to slip into a bad mood, my brain suddenly reminds me of the three of us laughing in the car over a fart joke and I smile. My first real cheerful moment since Mum and Dad split. I pull it out of my head, and tuck it away in my heart.

Mum and Dad had tried to make it sound easy. *These* are the days I'll be staying at the House on the Hill. *These* are the days I'll be at the Flat on the Flats. But second week in and already it's messed up 'cos I'm at Mum's on a Dad Night. I wonder if I have to stay the night or if Dad will come and get me. Ugh.

In case Yan asks any awkward questions, I tell her straightaway that this is *Mum's* place as opposed to *Dad's* place as my parents are divorcing. Although she nods like she understands, I know that she truly can't. When she looks at our temporary dining table and asks how many square centimetres it is, I wonder if she's calculating in her head if it would fit her family. I imagine them all sitting down for dinner together and, on the inside, I feel like a displaced person.

Yan looks with similar interest at the rest of the apartment, the view from the balcony and the inside of my bedroom from the doorway, even though there is not much to see.

"This is my first time to a friend's house," she says. "So, I'm really trying to store it in my long-term memory. Although..."

She turns to me.

"...do you know that memories don't actually exist? The brain doesn't remember anything, not like a computer does. It just creates a fantasy of what it thinks happened. How many times have you watched a movie, swearing something looked or happened a certain way, and you ended up being wrong?"

Yan reaches into her jacket pocket. "For example!" She pulls out the card with *White Rabbit cake* written on it and holds it up with the back facing me. "Tell me what's on the border of this."

Of course, I know the answer. I was there when Mrs Tagliatelle put in the special stationery order for it.

"Cupcakes with sprinkles."

"Are you sure?" Yan says, with raised eyebrows.

She's trying to psych me out. "Cupcakes with sprinkles," I repeat.

Yan flips it over and holds it up to my face.

The border is...

Slices of cake with sprinkles.

Oh.

How do you know someone hasn't travelled back into the past and changed it? my brain shouts at me.

Well, Occam's Razor. The simplest answer is often the best. That I remembered it wrong. And it makes more sense for the border to be cakes rather than cupcakes. It's a cake baking contest after all. I go to the kitchen where stuck to the overhead cupboard is the card that reads *Rocket cake.*

The border is slices of cake with sprinkles.

Mum brings us two hot Milos. They are the frothiest, tastiest, most chocolaty hot drinks ever. You can't tell she makes them in the microwave.

Yan looks at the teal sofa in my room and asks me where my bed is.

I unfold the sofa.

"But of course," she says. Like it's to be expected.

I fold the bed back into a sofa and we sit there with our hot Milos.

"What makes this thing so comfortable?" she asks me.

"Memory foam," I answer.

Yan nods and takes a sip of her Milo. Then she turns back to me. "Are you sure you want to go back in time? What if your memories aren't what you think they are? What if you only remembered the good bits and blocked out the bad bits?"

"My memories are real to me," I say firmly.

Yan nods again.

"Anyway, why do you want to know?"

"I'm just interested," she replies.

I sip my Milo and stare at her over the edge of the mug. She clears her throat.

"I travelled to a 1971 supermarket," Yan tells me.

"Yeah?"

"I went through the entrance and straight to the fresh fruit and vegetables display. Checked out the specials. Bananas were going cheap. Went up and down each aisle, looked at the tinned and packaged food. It's true, biscuits were bigger back then. Looked at what the other shoppers put into their carts. Tapped my feet to the supermarket music."

"You were using your time machine, weren't you?" I

say. I am doing what Mum calls "indulging someone".

"I found this amazing portal."

"Was it everything you thought 1971 would be like?"

Yan pauses. "There was a poster on a wall advertising a *7 Day Milk Diet.* I have no idea what it involves but... I don't think it involves pleasantness."

"Maybe some things are best left in the past," I say and surprise myself.

After that one good memory of laughing in the car, there are no more. Yan says she has to leave after her Milo. She asks if she can ring home so that someone can pick her up. Mum says she can drop her off. It turns out that Yan is not allowed to walk home from our place because she might get kidnapped.

I have not heard of anyone being kidnapped around here. I'm pretty sure Mum and Dad live in this area because some newspaper survey said it was the safest suburb in the state. It's as strange as...well, Mrs Chen believing she can't enter the Cake Competition because she won't be accepted.

I get into the back seat with Yan. She's quiet and doesn't say much.

We pull up to a small brick house that, instead of flower beds or a lawn at the front, has a kitchen garden. I look at the bamboo trellis with green beans creeping up it and trees with plastic bags tied around the unripened fruit to keep the birds away.

Yan has gone silent. Like she has shrunk, even though she's still the same size.

"See you tomorrow," she says in the smallest voice as she gets out of the car.

"Why isn't Yan allowed to walk home?" I ask Mum on the way back. "She's not going to get kidnapped. She's way too smart to take free lollies from a stranger in a van."

"I guess because she's never walked this way before," Mum replies. "Chinese mothers can be protective."

"You're not that protective," I point out.

"Your grandmother was," says Mum. "That's why I decided it was to end there."

I don't ask why Yan's house is back to front.

Dad comes over after he finishes work, so I guess I'm

going back over to the House on the Hill. Once again, he stands inside the doorway and doesn't come in any further.

"You didn't have to pick him up, you know," he says to Mum.

"The principal called. I thought it was important for me to," Mum replies.

"We'll have to disagree with some aspects of each other's parenting then." Dad sounds annoyed.

"Agreed," Mum snaps back.

I wish I could be anywhere but here right now. Like in the past.

"Let's get going, champ," Dad says to me.

"Don't forget this weekend is supposed to be my weekend!" Mum shouts as we're leaving. I hear the panic in her voice.

At Dad's place I write the apology I have to read out to Roscoe in front of the class. Even though Mum's told Dad about how I had to go to the principal's office, she hasn't communicated to Dad about the apology. And since Dad went to a different school as a kid, he doesn't know about Principal Taylor's tradition.

So, I write it in secret.

And I feel alone in secret, and I tell myself once again that, if it wasn't for my parents separating, I wouldn't have to feel this way.

1 WEEK 3 DAYS
7 HOURS 46 MINUTES
UNTIL GO LAUNCH

It's Tuesday morning and I've never felt gladder to have someone to walk to school with. Yan shows me what book she's got today – *Start Programming with the Electron, 1983* – and it makes me smile. It has a science fiction-looking cover with a clunky keyboard flying through a chaotic landscape of stars, planets and piano keys.

"Does it make any sense?" I ask.

"No," she replies.

"Then why are you reading it?"

"Because it's been scientifically proven that even if something doesn't make sense now, it doesn't mean it won't make sense in retrospect," replies Yan. "The mind is a mysterious and malleable machine! One that needs to be stretched! You should try it sometime."

"No thanks," I reply. It sounds painful.

"Well, don't blame me if you miss out on a subconscious clue that relates to something in the future!"

Yan knocks three times on the library door. "Do you want to see the portal to 1971?"

"Um, I have to be somewhere else this morning," I quickly say.

"Oh," replies Yan. "I guess I'll see you later then."

She looks disappointed. Even though all the days previously, she had entered the library by herself and had been fine about it.

The truth is, I'd love to hide myself inside the On the Way Out.

But I want to go straight to class so I can get the apology over and done with.

I don't tell Yan about the apology.

Not because I don't trust her. I just sometimes find it hard to share things.

Even though my apology isn't about how it feels to be caned, but instead is about how no one deserves to be called stupid, it's still horrible to read out loud.

I expect Roscoe to laugh and carry on, since the seats have rotated so he's directly opposite me again. But he looks uncomfortable. So does the rest of the class. Except for Miss Babette, who nods along with satisfaction on her face.

At lunch, I hang around the front office with Mrs Tagliatelle out of loyalty, because who else is going to help with the spell-checking of the all-important monthly school newsletter? It might go out with "too" instead of "to" and "there" instead of "their" and that would be a disaster.

Although the pile of *The Australian Women's Weekly Children's Birthday Cake Book* has almost sold out, there are still a few available and I have to keep an eye on them, especially when the phone lights up like Christmas during lunchtime. This is when all the parents ring up with their groans and gripes, and they don't consider that although they don't care about their lunchtime, maybe Mrs Tagliatelle would like to have hers.

My appetite is not how it normally is, but Mrs Tagliatelle sighs that the leftovers are going to go off if I don't help her eat them all, so I let her heap more on my plate.

I like the fact that these things in my life are still the same. That they are a constant in a world of unpredictable variables. Because life gets worse when...

1 WEEK 2 DAYS
4 HOURS 50 MINUTES
UNTIL GO LAUNCH

...at Wednesday lunchtime, Mrs Stonecutter comes back to the office. This time without Baby Violet. So she can put both hands on her hips, I guess.

"I've looked everywhere, and I cannot find the little pot and saucepan that is supposed to go on the Stove cake," she shouts, as if it's everyone else's fault. "And don't get me started on the tiny plastic plates!"

"I'm sorry, but the only cake we have left is the White Rabbit," Mrs Tagliatelle says firmly.

My heart skips a beat because I'm still hoping that Yan's mum will come in and put her name down.

"I don't want the White Rabbit! I already told you!" Mrs Stonecutter is having a tantrum like a three-year-old. I keep my head behind the computer screen, concentrating on the online stationery order I've been tasked with. It's obviously well overdue, as Mrs Tagliatelle's pen started running out of ink halfway through writing the list.

"We only allow one cake of each design to keep it interesting," replies Mrs Tagliatelle. "Otherwise, we'd have ten of the same Rocket cake."

"These cakes are so ugly anyway!" Mrs Stonecutter continues. "I've never seen them on Instagram!"

"Now, now. These cake designs have been beloved for generations." Mrs Tagliatelle tuts. "I dare say they're an Australian institution."

"The Duck cake is gross! It uses two potato chips for a beak, and let's not even mention the popcorn Mozart's wig on its head! The Clarence Clown looks like something Stephen King would have a bad dream about!"

"Look, your best option is to try to swap with a different parent," says Mrs Tagliatelle.

Mrs Stonecutter suddenly stops shouting. She goes stiff like a statue, and I can almost see the light bulb go off above her head. Without another word, she hurries out of the office. Mrs Tagliatelle and me both exhale at the same time.

"What do you think she's going to do?" I wonder out loud.

"Whatever it is, she's got the look of someone with a plan," says Mrs Tagliatelle.

I'm sure if Mrs Stonecutter has something in mind, it will be craftier than the patchwork dress on the Mary Jane cake.

I find out exactly what her plan is that evening.

I'm allowed to read a comic because I've done my homework, so I'm sitting at the wonky wooden fold-out table that's replaced the plastic trestle table. I ask Mum why she doesn't just go to a furniture shop and buy everything she needs, but Mum says she wants to slowly find things with "story" and "character". I personally think she's got coffee tables and footstools mixed up with books. She got the wooden table from an old gentleman up in the hills who told her he'd brought it all the way from London. It had been used down in the bunkers during the war.

Mum is practising her third trial cake. She's icing the body of the rocket with blue buttercream icing.

"Do you think real rockets are blue?" she asks, squinting down at *The Women's Weekly Children's Birthday*

Cake Book. "Would most rockets be covered in rainbow candy canes, chocolate chunks and fruit pastilles anyway?"

"Most rockets are white," I correct her. "To keep them as cool as possible. They can start to burn up exiting the atmosphere."

"Hmmm," says Mum.

She adds the final touch on the very top, a party hat. "How about that?" she asks.

I don't think most rockets have a rainbow-coloured nose either, but I say, "It looks awesome, Mum."

She looks surprised. Then delighted. "Let's see how it tastes, shall we? What about a big slice each for dessert?"

Now it's my turn to be surprised. You remember how I said Mum was dead against desserts?

She goes to get a knife.

There's a knock on the door and we both freeze.

Maybe it's Dad. But Dad knows that it's not his turn to have me until tomorrow.

Mum goes over to the door and opens it to reveal...

Mrs Stonecutter.

Oh no. The events from today at the front office quickly rearrange themselves in my mind, but too slowly for me to say anything before...

"Sophie!" Mrs Stonecutter gives Mum an air kiss on either side of her face and marches in. "So, this is the new place, huh? I do have a house-warming present for you, but I totally forgot it. Next time, I suppose!"

She sees the rocket sitting on the breakfast bar and her eyes light up.

"You're not attached to this cake, are you? Like *emotionally* attached?" Mrs Stonecutter says breezily and gives a little laugh.

"Umm..." says Mum slowly, as if she's trying to figure out why Mrs Stonecutter has come to visit if it's not to bring over the house-warming present that she has forgotten.

"How do you feel about swapping cakes, Soph?" says Mrs Stonecutter, cutting to the chase. "It's very important that I make this cake for Roscoe. You need to help *me*. Remember the times in the past when I helped *you*."

"Well..." says Mum, like she's trying to figure out what Mrs Stonecutter is talking about.

Then her face goes all soft. Like she can remember.

Oh no.

Mum's going to get sucked in. I've seen this before. Mrs Stonecutter has used this same tactic in the past to borrow shoes, the antique jade earrings that belonged to Mum's great-grandmother and, once, to drop Roscoe over for last-minute babysitting.

"You know about the tough patch we've been going through, what with Jason –" Mrs Stonecutter remembers I'm there and drops her voice "– and *you know*. That *Tax Accountant*. This will really cheer Roscoe up. You know how much my boy loves rockets."

"I guess it's just a cake."

I put my hand in the crook of Mum's arm to remind her to *stay strong*.

"Right? It's only a cake. So, I'll do the Rocket cake and you can have the Stove cake. I know you, Soph. You'll make the cutest Stove cake ever. We should catch up! I'll ring you!"

Mrs Stonecutter goes up to the kitchen cabinet, switches cards and then disappears at record speed, leaving Mum spinning in her wake. She didn't bother to ask how Mum was, or say congratulations on the new flat, or even try to make pleasant small talk about the weather.

She won't ring like she promised Mum. I'd be sus about catching up with her anyway. There was one time Mum got all dressed up because Mrs Stonecutter said they should go to this new celebrity chef cheese bar. Mrs Stonecutter cancelled at the last minute. I remember Mum silently changing out of her dress and high heels and brushing out the curls she'd put in her hair like it didn't matter. It must have, though, because Mum was quiet for three days afterwards.

I know they were best friends in primary school and Mum thinks that's worth holding onto, but she needs to leave that in the past.

Mum looks down at her beautiful Rocket cake and bursts into tears.

"It's okay, you don't need the Rocket cake," I say, and I really mean it.

The Stove cake is pretty cool. It's got two burners, one for a saucepan and the other for a pot, and a dish rack at the top to hold cups and plates. I know it's never made the number one position on my top ten list in any year, but honestly, there are one-hundred-and-seven cakes and I've only had eleven birthdays.

"I can't do anything right!" Mum says quietly, blowing her nose into the paper napkin I pass her.

She takes the party hat off the rocket, tips the cake sadly over on its side and slices it up with a bread knife.

She pushes a large piece on a saucer across the breakfast bar to me.

"It's delicious, Mum."

I guess I don't say this mushy stuff often because Mum's mouth pinches itself upwards in the corners and more tears form in her eyes.

"You make life worthwhile," she says.

Because Mum doesn't normally eat sugar, the thick slice of cake sends her over the edge. She opens up YouTube and says she's going to play me her favourite song from the first album she ever bought, which came out on CD. An embarrassing nineties video plays and she starts dancing around the room.

Even more embarrassingly, Mum grabs me by the hand and forces me to dance with her. I don't tell Mum that I last heard this song playing in the background of a dancing purple webpage from the past.

I don't mind this new version of Mum who eats cake and dances around a room. She even tries to dance with Helga the house plant, who has responded to her new home by growing flowers, when no one knew Helga was a flowering plant at all.

I look at her yelling, "It's just a cake! Stove cake –

woohoo!" and "There's more to life than cake!" while dancing at the same time, and I wonder if, one day, I'll look back at this very moment and remember it exactly the way I'm seeing it right now. I hope so.

THINGS THAT WILL NEVER HAPPEN AGAIN NOW THAT MY PARENTS ARE NOT TOGETHER

#6

For Mum's birthday last year, she wanted to go to the revolving restaurant thirty-three floors in the sky. We always do Mum and Dad's birthdays as a family, so I was very excited about going too. The previous year, Mum had chosen a picnic out on a farmstead in the middle of boring nowhere, and the year before that it was a tiny little box in the city that served blobs of spit on big white plates. Dad said it was technically called *foam* – aerated flavouring with a gelling agent – but even the science failed to thrill him as he was still hungry afterwards too.

Mum wore the same dress she'd worn to her Year Twelve ball. This wispy thing that shone like the surface of water, with a matching wrap. Dad wore a proper shirt with a tie, although being Dad, he wore his comfortable tan windbreaker instead of a suit jacket. Mum said I could wear what I wanted, so I wore a nice shirt and trousers. And, to impress Mum, a clip-on bow tie.

The view up in the restaurant was really cool. The floor to ceiling windows revealed a 360-degree night-time view that almost stretched to where we lived. But the restaurant was also old and the whole platform occasionally clunked while it spun everyone around. Mum kept telling Dad to stop running off to photograph the views and to eat his wagyu beef dinner, while she ordered a beetroot salad and picked at it.

I happily ate my creamy pasta until I recognized a loud voice coming towards us.

Oh no.

Mr and Mrs Stonecutter, along with Roscoe and Baby Violet, had arrived to sit at the table next to ours.

Mrs Stonecutter stood there, Baby Violet on her hip, and told Mum she looked too skinny. I wasn't half upset when the baby spewed milk down the front of Mrs Stonecutter's sparkly dress.

Mum smiled to be polite.

A guest walking towards us with a glass of wine was too busy admiring the view. That's when they lost their footing. Everything became slow motion. The glass of wine sailed through the air like space–time was bending. I'm pretty sure I'm right when I remember it spinning round and round like a firework.

I got up. Dad got up. But he was on the other side of the table. Mrs Stonecutter, in one smooth motion, hand-balled the baby to her husband and punched the wine glass out of the air like she was playing beach volleyball. Wine splattered on the front of Mum's beautiful dress.

"Oh, Sophie! Come with me, let's go fix ourselves up," said Mrs Stonecutter and they hastily fled to the women's bathroom. I couldn't believe Mrs Stonecutter had ruined Mum's high school ball dress. It was one of her most treasured possessions.

I continued eating and occasionally glared at Roscoe over at the other table, who glared back at me. Mum and Mrs Stonecutter took ages to come back, but when they did, they acted like nothing was the matter.

Even though Mum had a damp stain on her dress where the wine had mostly come off, she seemed a lot better and even managed to eat most of her salad. I was glad when Baby Violet started crying and the Stonecutter family had to leave without finishing their dinner.

The restaurant kept turning and Dad pointed out the location where he and Mum had first met. From thirty-three floors up, the world looked perfect.

The last part of the night turned out to be the best. I ordered a Baked Alaska Flambé for dessert because it sounded fancy and delicious – little did I know that the waiter was going to bring it over to the table and set it on fire in front of me. It was like a magic show and a science experiment at the same time. The blue flames toasted the meringue shell to a perfect yumminess before they mysteriously disappeared. Diners on the other tables turned around to stare and it was excellent to get so much attention.

Under the table, Mum and Dad held hands. I tried to pretend I didn't notice while I ate the ice cream inside my Baked Alaska Flambé, even though my ears turned hot.

Above the table, where you couldn't see the stain, Mum looked like a fairytale princess. She said she had Mrs Stonecutter to thank for saving the night, when it was Mrs Stonecutter who ruined it.

We definitely won't be doing family dinners for birthdays now. Mum and Dad can't even stand being in the same room together. Dad won't come inside the Flat on the Flats even though I really want to show him my new teal sofa bed.

1 WEEK 1 DAY
8 HOURS 50 MINUTES
UNTIL GO LAUNCH

I wish we all still lived back at the old house. Then I'd be able to walk down the hill every day with Yan. I'm thinking this as I approach school from Mum's...from the wrong direction. In my head, I picture a different universe where I get to do this, unaware of how lucky I am.

But then again, I didn't meet Yan until after my parents announced their separation, so maybe in that universe I'm still walking by myself. Unaware of how lonely I am.

Time and place and circumstances are complicated. The future is too huge and unknowable. Even the present is overwhelming. It would be much easier to go back to one moment in the past and exist in that for ever. Safe and predictable and perfect.

* * *

I've come to associate Science Week with being a bully and reading out an apology in front of the class. Before, I was the most unpopular kid in the class. Now it's even worse, I'm not even part of the group to be ranked any more. I'm an outsider.

When it's time to work on our posters, I'm glad not to be sitting next to Roscoe. But he's only separated by one other student on my right, so it's almost as bad.

I try to concentrate. Make a list of reasons why someone would want to travel back to the past.

To witness a historical event in real life. Possibly to check historical accuracy.

To avoid making a bad mistake. Like crashing their car.

To make a different life choice because they have regrets. To stop something bad from happening. Like a war.

Because things were better then.

There's a snort and of course it's Roscoe.

"What's so funny?" I hiss. As soon as it comes out of my mouth, I instantly wish I could turn back time.

"Laughing at my own joke, that's what." Roscoe glares. He tilts the corner of his poster towards me. "See. I've made a chart that grades the sorts of farts that will go into my Methane Car, like you get different grades of fuel at the petrol station."

Priscilla Chan, who is sitting between us, pulls her shoulders in uncomfortably.

"I'm sure you were laughing at me," I say firmly.

Roscoe cranes his neck over my work. "Reasons why someone would want to go back to the past? How about reasons why someone would want a fart car? Because it's a fart car! A fart car!"

Miss Babette is walking towards us. I hope she busts Roscoe.

Roscoe looks like he's hoping I'll get busted.

"Can I please move to a different desk?" asks Priscilla Chan.

"Can you boys please work quietly?" says Miss Babette. "Or you'll both be in trouble."

I'm not happy about this, but I go back to concentrating on my poster. I try imagining my time machine. It'll be white, to deflect heat like a rocket. Or maybe silver, that would provide even better insulation. Then I can cover my drawing of it in tinfoil. It'd look really excellent and shiny.

1 WEEK 1 DAY
1 HOUR 57 MINUTES
UNTIL GO LAUNCH

I know that Thursday is supposed to be a Mum Day. But for some mysterious reason (read: "adult" reason I can't possibly understand) my parents have decided to switch days. Just when I thought things were going to settle down, they hurl me back into space and I have to reorientate myself all over again.

I see Yan standing by the gate after school, a thing that has happened for the second time now; if it happens a third time it might be considered a constant.

She's in her green raincoat.

This is the first time it's rained all winter. Here, you kind of forget that it's winter and all of a sudden it starts to rain, and everyone is running around unprepared, getting wet. Except for Yan, who looks virtually waterproof.

I've got an umbrella because someone at school said umbrellas are cool and raincoats are not. Then someone else told me that at the other school in the same suburb, it's the other way around.

Who can keep up? Maybe I shouldn't even care.

But I think I do.

Disappointingly, I can't see what book Yan has today because it's tucked inside her raincoat, a rectangle against her chest.

"Are you going to your mum's?" asks Yan. "I'm just sticking around to say *see you tomorrow*. I've always wanted an opportunity to say it. Has a hopeful ring to it."

"Are you practising how to be a friend?" I blurt out.

"Yes," Yan admits.

"You don't have to try so hard," I reply. "And no. It's changed. I'm going to Dad's."

"Must be confusing," says Yan.

I feel like an untethered particle being bounced back and forth. Once we used to be a unit, now we are three pieces, like two paddles and a ball in an old arcade computer game.

"Can I walk with you then?"

I nod and we head out the gate together in the rain.

"How come I normally don't see you after school?" I ask, hoping she'll tell me this time.

Yan turns to me, her face small and round inside the hood of her green raincoat. "I go to Drama Club. There I can be free to move my body, use my voice, be my true self! But don't tell my mum."

I've never heard of anyone doing extracurricular school activities and trying to hide it from their parents. If I suddenly went to Drama Club, or STEM Club or even Boardgame Club, Mum would faint with happiness. I must have looked confused because Yan adds by way of explanation:

"I tell her I'm going to Extra Maths Club. But I made that up. It doesn't really exist."

"What's wrong with Drama Club?" I ask.

"She's scared I might become an actor." Yan laughs, but I can tell she doesn't think it's funny, and I don't either.

It also doesn't make sense to me, but then I think about Yan's mother, who believes Yan might get kidnapped after school and who grows vegetables in a garden at the front of their house, and none of that makes sense in my world either.

We reach the bottom of the hill and start the climb.

The backs of my calves burn. I guess I only walk up the hill two days instead of five days now, so I'm out of practice. I change the topic.

"What are you doing for your Science Week project?" I ask.

It's hard to tell because it's raining harder now and the hood of Yan's raincoat is the bulkiest thing I've ever seen, but I sense she's smiling.

"You know how they like to portray the future as everyone having sleek futuristic cars, wearing white, and it being so quiet it's almost Zen?"

She turns to me and I can see she's smiling. "Well, the future's not going to be leisurely living for sure, more like a hectic headache. If old people think life moves fast these days, wait till they see the future! Whee! It'll make their dentures fly out."

"See, I reckon that in the future when someone calls a ride-share it won't just be cars. It'll be flying trains, fifty-storey buses on legs that allow them to roller-skate over traffic jams, drones that can fit people inside, a sentient e-scooter...whatever can get you there the fastest! 'Cos the biggest poverty in the future will be time poverty!"

Yan is talking so animatedly that her hands with the fingerless gloves have come out of the pockets of her raincoat.

"I'm calling it *Uber Whateva* at the moment. But I'm trying to think of a jauntier name."

We reach the House on the Hill. It's only been a week, but already it looks different. The front garden is filling with weeds, the roses need to be dead-headed and the grass is getting long. It was Mum who used to do all that stuff, even the mowing.

I go to say bye, but Yan stands there on the footpath staring at the roof and the guttering as though it's of great interest to her. Which it probably is.

"Do you want to come inside?" I ask.

"Oh boy, would I like that," she replies.

I show her the hardcore safe where Dad stores the key and I let us in. Yan takes off her raincoat and reveals *The Book of Atari Software 1983*.

Tiger comes barrelling down the hallway and launches herself in the air. I catch *The Book of Atari Software* while Yan catches Tiger and holds her like a baby. Tiger twitches the tip of her tail and stays happily curved like the letter *C*.

She's never been good with strangers. "Have you met Tiger before?" I ask.

"No," replies Yan.

She must be lonely.

Yan looks around intently at everything, as though her brain is storing all this info to make a three-dimensional replica of the entire house later. She stares at the David Bowie poster on the back of my bedroom door and says, "I watched *Labyrinth* and it traumatized me. I don't think you're supposed to watch that movie until you're ready to come of age."

I'm embarrassed about it, but I show her my broken trundle bed, how my door clips the corner of it. Yan watches carefully, then puts Tiger down. She tries pushing the bottom bed under the top bed like everyone has done a hundred times before with no success.

"Forget about it," I say, ready to shoo her out of my bedroom.

"Do you have a screwdriver?" she asks. She's lifted up a corner of the mattress and is resting her face on the slats, looking deep inside the bed. She does the same on the other side.

I go to the kitchen and fetch the trusty red screwdriver from the third drawer. "Life is about choices. Once you figure that out, things get easier," says Yan.

She grips the screwdriver by the metal part and points to my window with its red handle. "How often do you open that?"

"Not often." I shrug. "Maybe a few times a year when it gets really hot."

There's no flyscreen behind the glass so I don't want mozzies getting in. Or robbers, as a matter of fact.

"You would say it's more important that your bed slides in and out than the window being able to open?"

I nod.

"Then the choice is made," Yan replies, in the most solemn tone I've ever heard anyone use. Like she's delivering a speech at a funeral.

Wait, I think, *I've changed my mind. Whatever it is, don't do it...*

Yan unscrews something out of my bed frame. She

drops it into my palm and, as I try to figure out what it is, she...

...takes my whole window out. Unscrews something out of the bottom of it and screws it into my bed. She pushes the trundle and it...

...slides back under the bed like it's supposed to. Like magic.

"How...?"

"The wheel mechanism was broken on one side," she says. "I replaced it with the one in the window."

She puts my window back into the frame.

"How did you know how to do that?"

"From absorbing information, I guess," replies Yan, as if she herself thought it was magical and mystical. "You know how I was saying that the mind is a mysterious machine?"

"But even my dad and mum couldn't see the problem," I say.

I look at the broken wheel in my hand. It will go into my special shoebox.

"Sometimes you need fresh eyes. A different point of view," replies Yan. "Now, I'd really like a refreshment if you have anything to offer?"

*   *   *

I get two Ribena juice boxes out of the fridge and take Yan to the Man Cave. Tiger looks expectantly at the juice boxes, realizes she's not human, shakes her head and follows.

In the darkness, the lights of the sixteen computers look like they are blinking out a message. Yan watches them as if she understands and can decode what they are trying to say. I don't want to ruin the experience by turning on the blinking and possibly exploding ceiling light, so I go over and turn on the desk lamp instead.

It illuminates the room to reveal that Dad might have pushed the last piece of ceiling back in, but a piece in the middle is now dangling precariously loose above Pop's motorcycle.

"Ah. A vehicle of the future. A fellow time machine," says Yan, staring at it as if she knows. "For two travellers."

"It's just a motorcycle. A vehicle from the past," I insist, and I show her the tiny helmet I've been making for Tiger out of the polystyrene ball. "For three travellers hopefully."

Yan tries positioning the helmet on Tiger's head. Unusually, Tiger sits still and patiently. But it falls off.

"You need to cut ear holes into this thing," she says.

I steer her away towards the computers. "You'll like this."

Somehow it feels like I'm presenting her with a gift, because I know her well enough to say so. Because I remembered the joy in her voice when she found a portal to a 1971 supermarket.

I turn on Dad's personal computer and try the password I know.

It hasn't changed. It's still *Sophie#2006*.

I show Yan how the time machine, like hers, can take data back to any point in time in the past. She watches thoughtfully, as I take time back to the day when we hiked Reabold Hill. I show her the photos and the short video where Dad says, "Well done! That's my Little Man!" and Mum shouts, "I told you! I told you!" I am transported back into that moment again. I remember the heat, the smell, the sky. What I was thinking. How I felt.

I thought it would be sad, like when I last looked at it with Dad, but with Yan there, it doesn't feel so bad.

I end up telling her, as we sit in the two high-backed swivel chairs, about how awful it was a week ago when my parents told me they were getting divorced. About how I know it wasn't their intention, but it felt like they were ganging up on me. And how at that point my whole world became a black hole, and I was doing my best not to get sucked inside. Which was hard as I felt my entire life had been ripped away and I was now floating, untethered, lost. Major Tom unable to connect with Ground Control.

Before I know it, I'm telling Yan about the six memories that mean the most to me, that happened before my parents split. I thought she would tell me that *memories aren't real, they're just fantasies*, but she doesn't judge me and instead listens.

Once in a while, as it all comes spilling out, she asks me when a certain thing happened. And I can tell her the exact time and date because in my mind each memory is as vivid and clear as if it had happened yesterday.

I see her scribble down some things on an empty page of Dad's notepad.

When I tell her about how my parents worked together to comfort me after the whole "Space Oddity" incident, that's when the tears come spilling down my face. Yan picks up the box of tissues without missing a beat and passes it to me.

From inside her schoolbag she produces a plastic

packet and places it on the desk. It glows neon pink. She opens it and passes me something soft, wrapped within a frilled paper casing.

"This is something only strawberry mochi can fix. Trust me, I know. Put it in your mouth, it'll make you feel better."

I do, and it's delicious. A soft chewy strawberry explosion that lights up the room.

I blow my nose and say, "That's it. Story of my life."

As we sit there, facing the sixteen computers all whirring and blinking, it's as if we're in command of a control centre and we're ready for lift-off.

"I'm sorry about your 'Space Oddity' incident," she says.

"Sorry about your *Labyrinth* incident," I blurt out.

We look at each other and laugh in the same language of growing pains and coming of age.

"I have to go home now," replies Yan, standing up. "My mum will be at the door waiting. Or standing by the front window lifting the lace curtain every five seconds."

I get up too and turn on the ceiling light.

The fluorescent tube flickers and flickers and shocks itself into life, and the room becomes a sharp white box.

Even though I was expecting it, it still hurts my eyes. The magic that was there before is gone.

"What does your mum need you so badly to do?" I ask.

"Violin practice," replies Yan.

I think back to how Yan said her mum wouldn't let her do drama in case she became an actor. "So, your mum wants you to become a classical musician?"

"No, don't be silly," replies Yan. "Of course she doesn't."

I look in wonder as my new friend puts on her giant green raincoat and tucks *The Book of Atari Software 1983* inside, safe against the drizzling rain.

Yan suddenly stops and turns back to me.

"I now understand your Human Condition," she says, putting her hand over her heart. "You will hear further from me about *Mission Major Tom*."

She bows and hurries off.

I don't know about any mission, let alone *Mission Major Tom*.

Until I go back to the Man Cave to look for the rest of the strawberry mochi. Sadly, Yan must have taken it with her. But what I do find is her scribblings on Dad's notebook.

Which are:

04:129:23:00
00:250:05:00
00:360:00:20
00:360:05:45
00:347:21:06
00:249:22:22

"That was Mum. She really wants to make sure she gets you this weekend."

Dad has hung up the phone, but he's still holding onto it as though it might attack. Mum's voice was a *bit* loud on the other end.

"I'll miss you," says Dad.

I don't know what to say, so I don't say anything.

Dad stands there looking awkwardly back at me, like he doesn't know what to do either. "Oh, I just remembered. Deconstructed Dessert time."

He hurries off into the kitchen, sounding relieved, and I'm relieved as well that he's found something to do. Without Mum to order him around or give him a task like chop an onion or boil spaghetti, he seems lost. On the other

186

hand, Mum, without her sous chef, has found freedom in a slow cooker, where she throws anything in, leaves it for eight hours and everything comes out tasting the same.

A mug is shoved into my hand. In it is sponge cake, chocolate biscuits, chocolate sauce, whipped cream, and hundreds and thousands. Dad sits down on the couch next to me.

"What are *you* going to do this weekend?" I ask.

"I'm going to meet some friends at the sports bar," he replies, taking a spoonful of Deconstructed Dessert.

I have never known Dad to watch sports on the small screen by himself, let alone on a big one with screaming fans.

"Are you there to find a lady friend?" I say out of the side of my mouth. I make a face.

"Hmm?" Dad looks genuinely surprised at my question and the glasses almost fall off his face. "I was hoping for a chicken parmigiana meal. With chips instead of a salad."

After we finish Deconstructed Dessert, Dad says he's going to work on Pop's motorcycle. Normally, I would use my

TV privileges this time in the evening, but instead, I go to the Man Cave too.

I guess I'm trying to find my place in this new arrangement. After the explosion of our lives, the pieces blasted into space are still falling into their new positions. And maybe I can choose the places where they land this time.

Dad is cleaning some parts of the motorcycle and greasing others, and he's trying to teach me, even though it's not my sort of thing. I hold the polystyrene helmet in my hand and start carving out the holes for Tiger's ears. Dad passes me a can of silver spray paint and says I can use it on the helmet after I've finished. Tiger sits in the sidecar and supervises, twitching her tail.

This is better than watching TV.

Later in the night, I show Dad how my trundle bed now works again. Like a typical adult, he says, "I could have fixed that."

He drifts off to settle into bed and read the latest edition of *The Curiosity Room* magazine. I'm finally able to close the door of my bedroom. I lie down on the mattress that I know still has a boot print under the fitted sheet, and I stare up at the poster of David Bowie.

I think of Dad, reading about how scientists have discovered that Jupiter is big because in the past it swallowed micro planets in its path like a Pac-Man. I think about Mum, letting go of things because they are "just cake". I think about Yan practising the violin for no clear reason other than she has to.

I listen to the rain and I think of each of us as a coordinate and about the space between us. Tonight, we do not seem so far apart.

It stops raining the next morning. I say bye to Dad and head out before he does, which is my new routine when I'm at the House on the Hill. Yan is standing outside on the footpath, like she does now. She has her green raincoat on even though the sun has come out. I can tell she's got a new book tucked inside it.

"What old computer are you learning about this time?" I ask. "I still don't get why you do it?"

It's not so much a question than it is…

Banter.

Like a "thing" between friends.

"As I have said numerous times, James, knowledge is interconnected," Yan replies, rolling her eyes. "Just like life and the world and the universe *and* the metaverse and you and me."

"Let me see it then."

Yan slides the book out of her raincoat.

It's...*101 Albums You Should Listen to Before You Go.*

"I've also learned it pays to not be predictable." Yan grins at me.

For my project I've imagined the time machine as a high-backed chair with a monitor in front of it, hooked up to thirteen computers. Carefully I embellish the whole thing with the tinfoil I've bought from home. I'm glad that, for today, Roscoe and his farts are sitting far, far away from me.

I cut a fresh rectangle out of white card and stick it onto my poster.

How A Time Machine Might Work
Did you know that some computers have backup software called a Time Machine? It makes sure that you don't lose anything you store on your computer, including all your personal data such as photos,

music, emails, documents and other media. The Time Machine can take you back to any time in the past and show you what everything looked like at that exact point.

I pause and chew on the end of my pencil.

A Swedish philosopher named Nick Bostrom came up with the theory that we might be living in a computer simulation. If all humans and everything we know are just part of a software program and we can harness the ability to control this program, then we too should be able to go back in time.

I find myself hyperaware all of a sudden, looking at everything in the classroom carefully, as if I might see any glitches or lags that you might notice when the computer processor occasionally packs up.

Like I too have X-ray eyes.

Like I have unlocked something.

Now I know why Yan looks into bushes, scrutinizes the existence of power poles and so carefully examines random cats. Maybe we're both trying to find the cracks that will explain why we live in a mad world where mums make kids practise violin for no reason, dads unveil entire motorbikes you never knew about, and parents break up.

Recently, a young inventor by the name of Yan Chen created a time machine with a proxy inside that allows you to request any webpage in the form it existed at any point in time. This is of historic value as it allows anyone to look through the eyes of an internet user from the past. Perhaps this same principle can one day be expanded beyond the internet.

On the other side of the room, I see Roscoe get up from his desk and go to the bin at the front of the class. He empties out his pencil sharpener even though I can see it's not even full. Then he purposely takes the long way back to his desk by walking past me.

"It's *Science Week*, you know," he says under his breath. "Not *Fantasy Week*."

I pretend not to hear him and cut out another bit of cardboard. I plan revenge in my head where I go and empty my pencil sharpener, walk past him and say, "It's *Science Week*, not *Joke Week*."

But I don't do it.

Yet another drama unfolds at the front office at lunchtime. I'm helping Mrs Tagliatelle with one of the most important tasks of the year – making the display labels for the Summerlake Primary School Cake Competition that is only two weeks away now – when a mystery parent walks in.

I've never seen him before. But he's dressed in the way men in the movies do when they're off to play golf.

"I'm here with regard to the Rocket cake," he says. "Who do I talk to?"

"You can talk to us," says Mrs Tagliatelle and puts a hand on my shoulder. I like how she includes me.

"But the Rocket cake is no longer available," Mrs Tagliatelle continues with a firm voice. "As I've told another parent, your best bet is to try to swap with whoever has the Rocket cake."

"Why can't we make whatever cake we want?" The man's voice starts to get loud. "Why are you policing the cakes like this?"

"We're trying to make the competition interesting." Mrs Tagliatelle sighs.

"Whoever has the Rocket cake is going to win! It's won the last two years in a row! This competition is rigged!"

The man leaves, slamming the glass door as hard as he can, but luckily the door has a pneumatic arm, so it comes to a nice soft close.

Mrs Tagliatelle rubs her face and makes a painful noise like a wounded cat.

"Should I go and tell the security guard in case he's lurking outside?" I ask her.

"There's no need, pet," she answers. "Some parents take these things way too seriously. I heard that poor Mr Fernandez's left eye is still not right after he volunteered to umpire the kids' baseball game over the weekend and a parent had a go at him."

I concentrate on making the display labels as best as I can.

Mrs Tagliatelle has given me a whole bunch of blank cards, except these are twice the size of the ones used for the cake names. I check the border and it's the same – slices of cakes with sprinkles. I find myself turning the cards over, so the blank sides face upwards.

Pausing.

Turning them back the right way.

The border is still made of slices of cakes with sprinkles.

I sigh in relief.

Carefully, I copy from the ancient, frosting-encrusted Cake Entry Book using my neatest handwriting.

Cake Name. Parent or Guardian Name.

Ginger Neville. Zoe Walton.

I check that there are no spelling errors and that I have spelt the name correctly before I move onto the next cake. Soon I am working in a satisfying rhythm.

Pink Elephant. James Foley.

Jungle Elephant. Heather Waugh.

To my surprise, where there should be a blank is:

White Rabbit. Anonymous.

"Mrs Tagliatelle," I ask, "did someone actually come in and register for the White Rabbit cake?"

"They did, pet!" she exclaims in response. "But whoever came in did so while neither you nor I was at the front desk. One of the temps took the money but forgot to take their details."

I wanted to ask if the temp had said anything about

what this contestant looked like, but I'm guessing that would be rude.

"Isn't that lovely for the White Rabbit? To be chosen after all. Bless its little desiccated coconut paws!"

I like how Mrs Tagliatelle treats the rabbit like it's real and deserves respect. I'm glad that every single cake has been selected, because whoever has chosen theirs has done so for a reason. In a universe that Dad says is cold and uncaring and only exists for the sole purpose of doing so, it is nice to know there is love. Even if it's just for a school cake baking competition.

1 WEEK 0 DAYS
1 HOUR 59 MINUTES
UNTIL GO LAUNCH

The rest of the day turns out to be like a regular summer's day even though it is winter. The weather is warm. Everyone moves around a little slower, including all the teachers. Yan has shed her green skin and hurries up to me as I wait at the school gate for her after school, the copy of *101 Albums You Should Listen to Before You Go* grasped in her arms.

"We must prepare for Mission Major Tom," she says breathlessly. "I have to run preliminary tests. It's like when you launch anything, really. A rocket. A satellite. A book. A time machine is no different."

Oh. She must be talking about her internet time machine. We reach the bottom of the hill and I mentally prepare the back of my legs for the journey upwards.

"Okay," I say.

Even though I still have no idea what she's really talking about.

Having watched Mum and Mrs Stonecutter's "friendship", I have realized that what is important in a real friendship is balance. As Dad says, it has been observed in the known universe that if two stars of the same size come into orbit, they will dance together. But if a star comes into contact with, say, *a black hole*, then it will get *sucked up in a second*.

I'm trying to dance with Yan by humouring her.

"Oh, good," replies Yan. "I wasn't sure if you'd be cool with it or not."

I've figured it out. Yan is going to dial the coordinates of the six most important memories of my life in her black box and we're going to see how the internet looked at those precise times. But first she's going to show me some other (presumably awesome) things – these *preliminary tests* – before the big reveal.

I'm cool with that. In fact, I feel grateful. She's obviously trying the best she can for me with what she has. Because she is a good friend.

We ascend the hill and I look up into the sky and feel

the sun on my face.

For a moment I'm almost as happy as I used to be.

We sit in the two high-backed swivel chairs with our cartons of Ribena. The piece of ceiling in the middle of the room hangs lower over Pop's motorcycle. Yan puts her Ribena down and picks up the polystyrene helmet.

I finished carving it last night, ear holes and all. I just haven't sprayed it silver yet. Yan fits it over Tiger's head. I expect Tiger to flatten her ears and try to shake it off. But she doesn't. She continues sitting regally on Yan's lap with the helmet on, a perfect fit, twitching the tip of her tail like a villain's accomplice in a movie.

When Yan dips her hands into her schoolbag, I'm hoping she's got more of that strawberry mochi, but she brings out the black box with the big dial in the middle and the small digital screen. The internet time machine.

"Is it okay if I use this one?" she says, indicating Dad's personal computer.

"Yeah," I reply, and she takes out an ethernet cable and connects them.

"Now, I need you to understand that the coordinates

don't matter as much because it's only a preliminary test," says Yan. "So, don't get all hung up on that."

She turns on the internet time machine and I watch as the display panel lights up.

"Look!" Yan points to the monitor.

Dad's Time Machine software has automatically popped up.

"They've detected each other. Isn't that cute?"

I try not to pull any faces. After all, Yan treating technology like it's human because it can make a connection is like me treating cakes as living things because they have eyes and smiles (even if they're only Smarties and piped icing).

"Now, let me choose a random coordinate," says Yan. "I should have thought of this when I built the thing! To put in a random coordinate generator. Oh well."

I watch as Yan closes her eyes and twists the dial all the way around three times. The numbers on the screen start spinning so fast that they become a neon-green blur. Slowly the digits stop one by one at:

25:129:23:00

"Whoa," says Yan. "I might have spun that a bit too hard."

I try to remember if the internet existed twenty-six years

ago, in *1997*. If it did, it would have been extremely basic. I try to imagine what type of technology they had back then.

Something pops up on the computer monitor.

We both turn at the same time. It's not very big, so we both lean in, almost bumping heads.

It's a photo.

Slightly fuzzy. Of a rolling green field of yellow flowers.

"I know what this is," I say. "Dad told me that in 1997 he bought his first digital camera. It cost eight-hundred dollars and had a resolution of 1.3 megapixels. Although 8K Ultra HD was still two decades away, he said that it made him feel like he was living in the future."

"Excellent! This photo will make a perfect preliminary test because it doesn't have people in it," replies Yan. "If it did, then we'd have to talk about what happens if you do something to accidentally change the past and therefore change the space–time continuum and the future itself aaaaand that's a whole other kettle of fish when it comes to physical time travelling."

"Excuse me?" I say.

I thought she just said *physical time travelling*.

"Are you ready?" asks Yan.

"Ready for what?" I ask.

"Is this not what you said you wanted?"

Yan confirms the coordinates on the internet time machine.

"I thought it was only an internet time machine," I say.

Yan gives me a *have-you-not-learned-anything* look. "What was I saying about memories being unreliable! Did I ever call my time machine an *internet* time machine?"

Umm…

"Anyway," she adds. "We can argue about that later. Let's go!"

The dodgy light above us starts to flicker. There is a strange humming noise. Time suddenly s l o w s.

I lift my hand up to touch my face and it seems to take a long time to get there. I try to turn my head towards Yan, but that seems to take for ever as well.

Out the corner of my eye, at normal speed, I watch as the piece of ceiling finally falls on top of Pop's motorcycle. But since it's only made of felt and foam, it lands gently and then slides onto the floor.

All of a sudden –

The sound of nothing.

Not even of silence, because silence is itself a thing.

Then…

25:129:23:00

Sun on my face.

I open my eyes.

Yan is beside me.

And so is Tiger, wearing her unfinished polystyrene helmet. She spots a butterfly in the long grass and goes bouncing off.

My arms, legs, my entire body are moving again at a normal speed. No flickering ceiling light. No humming noise. No Man Cave. Just me and Yan standing in a field of long, green grass and yellow flowers and a perfect blue sky. The breeze gently blows, tugging at the corner of my school shirt. Tugging at the ends of Yan's black hair. Everything has a hazy lo-fi quality.

"Like I told you once before..." she says. "Sometimes I dream about living inside a wistful-looking photo. So, isn't this a treat?"

"We're in Dad's photo from 1997?"

Yan spreads out her arms. Silently her mouth forms the words *ta-da*! She doesn't need to say more.

I wonder where Dad took this photo. It's not a place I've seen before. It could be overseas. It could be in a different state or it could be down the road. All I know is that twenty-three years ago Dad wasn't together with Mum; hadn't even met Mum yet. He had bought a digital camera, put some belongings into a backpack and ventured away from home by himself for the very first time.

And it's like I can feel his emotions when he took the photo. Wondering. Unsure.

Lonely. But also, excited. Free. Hopeful.

"Don't look so serious!" Yan says and tugs at my elbow.

She lies down flat on the grass and I join her. Tiger is back in her arms.

"Maybe I should use the time machine for more than internet browsing," Yan ponders to herself.

The breeze blows and the grass shimmers.

"I understand what you want, James," she says to me. "I can see it now."

And just when I thought that maybe I could stay in this picture for ever, I hear...

That humming noise again.

The sky is replaced by a flickering light on a ceiling.

The thick, soupy feeling that time is about to s l o w down again.

And...

We're back.

"Ouch!" The hand I'd been lifting up to my cheek suddenly slaps me in the face.

"Looks like the preliminary test was a success," says Yan with sweat on her brow and a smile on her face. "We were there for exactly four minutes twenty-six seconds. But next time, I will drop you off by yourself and for ever."

"For ever?"

"Yes, otherwise known as 'eternal' or 'everlasting'. Defined as a perpetual state in which—"

"I know what for ever means, Yan!"

I guess Mum would call this a *plot twist*.

"It's settled then. Let's pick a date for Mission Major Tom! What are you doing in exactly one week's time?"

"The strangest thing happened today," Mum tells me as we walk up to her apartment. "There was this man lurking around the car park on campus at my work."

Mum had been very tense when she stood on the doorstep of the old house. She'd come to pick me up this evening instead of waiting until tomorrow morning, which is what was agreed. She looked ready to fight Dad over it.

"Security was called because they thought he had a weapon," continues Mum. She slides in the key. "But it didn't turn out to be a weapon. It was a bread roll. Possibly his lunch. You can't arrest someone for carrying a bread roll."

Mum twists the key and I turn the doorknob because her other hand is holding a shopping bag. I wonder how

Mum opens the door by herself when I'm not around.

"Then, as suddenly, the man disappeared. I didn't see him myself, but apparently he was dressed in golfing clothes. Maybe he went to play golf. They never found out who or what he was after."

We tumble inside and Mum puts the bag up on the breakfast bar. I stand in the middle of the room and through the glass sliding door I can see two yellow chairs out on the balcony.

"Daryl at work gave them to me," says Mum. She blushes and puts her hands on her cheeks. "They were just taking up room in his garage."

We both get changed into our pyjamas and Mum starts making a practice version of her new cake. She bakes a large flat butter cake in a lamington sponge tray and then cuts it into three sections. One piece for the back of the stove. Two pieces stacked in front for the oven and cooktop. The pieces refuse to stand upright. But once Mum covers the whole thing in a layer of icing, they have no choice but to stick together.

She then shows me what's inside her shopping bag.

It's a doll's set of kitchenware. With plates, saucers, a saucepan and a frying pan. That's why Mum didn't see the man in the car park. She went to the shopping centre behind the university campus that has a toy store in it.

"Do you think the Stove is a lame cake?" Mum asks, worry in her voice.

I look up from *101 Albums You Should Listen to Before You Go*. Yan had shoved it into my hands before she left.

"Just because it got picked second-last doesn't make it a lame cake," I reply.

"Hmm," says Mum.

"It's got strengths that the other cakes don't have. Like the cuteness factor of having sausages made out of chocolate bullets and a fried egg made out of a white marshmallow and a yellow smartie."

"Hmm," says Mum.

Mrs Tagliatelle is right when she says parents take silly school competitions way too seriously. Every parent wants to make the Rocket cake, every parent wants to win first prize, every parent wants to win their kid's love.

"The point of the cake competition isn't to win anyway," I say. "It's to fundraise."

"Huh!" says Mum.

After she checks the cake using a level tool that I'm sure belongs to Dad, and trials the placement of the little utensils, she makes a cuppa and jumps onto the couch. She stretches her legs and takes a huge breath out.

"Can I ask a question?" I ask.

"I like questions," says Mum.

"I was wondering why..." I start and stop.

"It's okay," says Mum. "I don't mind answering a tough question. It's much better than you asking, *What happens if a black hole comes into proximity with another black hole*, and me replying, *I have not the faintest clue.*"

"I just want to know why you never made a cake for the Summerlake Primary School Cake Competition in the past!" I blurt out.

My face goes red and then my ears grow hot.

"Are you disappointed in me?" Mum asks.

Well.

"There are no excuses from me, James. I'm sorry."

She pauses.

"I was like you once." Mum smiles sadly to herself. "When I was little, I used to pore over that book and choose the cakes inside my head. I'd wish that your Ah Ma would bake one for my birthday but—"

"— she couldn't. She didn't feel like it was part of her world," I finish, without realizing I'd opened my mouth.

"I find I'm repeating the same thing. Sometimes cycles can be hard to break," Mum continues. "But, I'm breaking it now. I'm making this cake for you."

I wish I could say thank you, but it doesn't come out, because I've always found it hard to share my feelings. So, I can understand how hard it is to try to change something when everything has been a certain way for your whole life.

After Mum serves another slow-cooked meal that tastes exactly the same as the last one, I flip through *101 Albums You Should Listen to Before You Go* and make notes of the ones I'm actually going to listen to.

"What have you got there?" asks Mum.

I let her turn the pages. She talks enthusiastically again about music and high school, about the one time she snuck out with friends to a concert, which I'm honestly hearing for the first time.

She goes to YouTube to show me the song she stood up in her seat and danced to, but after it finishes, another video starts to play automatically.

It's this particular duet Mum always plays when she's in a certain mood. You can tell the studio version of the song was dubbed on top of the grainy old concert footage because the singers' mouths don't quite match up to the words. Mum likes it because the man holds hands with the woman and, at one point, spins her around in a dance. Puts his arms around her and rocks her from behind. At the end he gets down on his knees and kisses the back of her hand.

"Do girls actually like that stuff?" I mumble.

"No," replies Mum. "It's all for show, don't you realize? Tommy loved a man in real life and I'm sure Sally had a husband."

"Then why do you like watching it?" I ask.

"Because I like the fantasy," Mum replies. She smiles a deliriously happy smile and takes a sip of her sleepy oat flower tea. When the video clip ends, she puts it on again.

I watch the fake couple and pretend they don't look like my parents in happier times.

I think about living inside the perfect memory for ever. Where all I'll ever know is within the constraints of that memory, my entire world never extending beyond that.

Like Mum living in the moment for that four minute and eighteen second video. Then clicking *replay*.

I think about Mission Major Tom counting down.

It rains all of Saturday. I learn about the one-hundred-and-one albums I should listen to before I go. Mum experiments with the fluffiness factor of different frostings. But as soon as there's a break in the weather on Sunday morning, Mum hurries us out of the apartment and we go up the coast, rent two e-scooters at the hut there, and then we're whizzing down the bike path.

It's *freezing*. The faster you go the colder it is. Not that I can go fast, anyway, in this bulky yellow raincoat that Mum has made me wear. I look like a deep-sea fisherman. Ten minutes in and Mum is way ahead. I shout at her to slow down, but the wind whips my words away, and then it starts to rain. And not just rain – it pours.

Up ahead I can see Mum suddenly brake. It's lucky

that she's got one of those scooters with the fancy colourful lights or else I wouldn't be able to see her at all. I tell her we should head back, but Mum is upset that we paid for two hours and it's only been ten minutes. She thinks the rain will pass. The only thing that changes her mind is when she starts thinking that since the scooters are electric, we might get electrocuted.

Science will never be Mum's strong point.

We end up back in the car, drenched and holding paper cups of hot chocolate to our lips.

"I'm sorry," says Mum.

"What are you sorry for?" I ask.

"I wanted to make this weekend count."

"I don't need to be constantly entertained; I'm growing up, you know," I reply. "Anyway, there will be *more weekends*."

Even though I know that is a lie.

I know adults say not to tell lies, but it appears that *white lies* or *lies to make someone feel better* are exceptions.

Mum smiles and deposits her hot chocolate into the cup holder.

I put my hand over her hand.

Mum looks more shocked than surprised, but she doesn't move her hand away.

I wonder if in the future I will look back on this moment and laugh and say, "Do you remember the time we got caught out in the rain on our electric scooters and you thought we would electrocute ourselves? The hot chocolate sure tasted the best after."

But if I go in Yan's time machine, I will never know the future.

We spend the rest of Sunday inside. I borrow Mum's computer to stream an album from the list of one-hundred-and-one albums I should listen to before I go. It's by David Bowie and it's about a rock'n'roll alien called Ziggy Stardust who comes to earth from Mars and wows everyone with his awesomeness before leaving all his fans behind.

I've relocated a few of my things from the other house, like my Lego Lunar Space Station, my Newton's Cradle and my night-light. The bedroom is starting to feel like home. It's a shame that I'll be going soon.

Mum's in the kitchenette mixing buttercream icing to get it the right colour for a vintage stove, a colour she says is called duck-egg blue. Dad would probably be outraged if he was around, because he would say that sounds *unscientific* and that colours should be referred to using the assigned code in a subtractive colour model. But Dad is not around and there's just the sound of Mum humming the love song from *Back to the Future*.

"So, did Dad say what he's doing without you there?" she asks.

"Going to the sports bar with his friends."

There's no expression on Mum's face to indicate anything in particular. Then all of a sudden...

"I get so lonely when you're not around!" Mum drops her spatula and looks at me. "Oops. I shouldn't have said that."

I shrug.

"I've never lived by myself before! I'm still adjusting! Not that it doesn't mean I don't miss you, regardless."

"I'm proud of you, Mum," I say.

I can't believe I said that. You know how I get about the googly gushy stuff. But I mean it.

Mum smiles so big it looks like her face might crack.

And for a moment I think maybe I don't need to go back to the past.

Maybe Mum would also call that a *plot twist*.

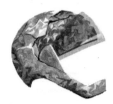

At school, I don't see Yan at all. Even on Wednesday, when the classes all go to the undercover area for assembly, she keeps her head down and stares at the concrete. I almost raise my hand to catch her attention, but she doesn't seem to sense me in her orbit. So, I don't.

She shouldn't have a reason to avoid me...right?

In class, I put the final touches on my Science Week poster. I have one last information box to make.

The Unintended Dangers of Time Travel

You might accidentally change the future for the worse – e.g. you stop two people from meeting

You might accidentally cause the end of the world – e.g. you try to stop a war and it leads to nuclear annihilation

You go into the past and find you cannot come back

You might start to think things will be better in the future

I'm quite pleased with my work. I give the foil bits a polish with the sleeve of my fleece jacket. Even if Roscoe came over and spat on it, he can't take the shine off how I'm feeling. In a way, my poster is like a farewell card I'm leaving behind.

I'm sad, though, when I see Mrs Tagliatelle at lunch. But it's super busy because Principal Taylor is hosting The Great Australian Principals Afternoon Tea and there are lots of name badges I have to double-check the spelling for. And I have to make sure the tags that read *gluten-free*, *vegan* and *sugar-free* are correct or else we could have a dietary disaster on our hands.

As soon as that is done, I leave so I can go and say goodbye to the librarians, even though they have no idea why I'm doing that. When I get there, they are arranging the Science Week posters from our class on the display boards.

Yan isn't there.

She's not hiding in her nest among the On the Way Out or between any of the shelves.

I ask the Head Librarian where she is and Ms Page says, "Yan dropped by, but she was uncharacteristically not in the mood to be at the library, and she took off."

I try looking for her around the school, but I don't find her by the time the bell rings. Maybe because I'm only half-hearted about it.

Thursday morning. The custody parameters have shifted once again. I ended up staying the night at Mum's and after school I will go straight to Dad's.

"The days go past so fast," Mum says to me as she sips a cup of tea, still in her dressing-gown.

The days catch me by surprise too. It feels like time is shorter when you have two separate lives to fit in. But come tomorrow, I won't have to worry any more about things changing and, just as I get used to it, changing once again.

Come tomorrow, Mission Major Tom will take me away, back into the past where everything will stay the same.

I'll have to be careful to choose the right memory.

What if I can't choose between any of them because I like them all?

Maybe I need to talk to Yan about that random generator.

"I guess it's your dad's turn to have you this weekend," Mum comments sulkily and then sniffs. "I bet you anything the weather is going to be perfect."

Spontaneously, I give her a hug.

"What was that for?" she asks.

"Nothing," I reply.

I study Mum carefully, like Yan studies people. I know that it's only been two weeks since my parents broke up, but the Mum from back then and this Mum right now are different people. They are only different in small ways, but enough to matter. And there is lots to like about this Mum.

I look around at the apartment. It doesn't look so drab and depressing now that Mum has filled it with a personality that I never knew she had inside of her. Colourful charity shop artworks decorate the walls and a curved wicker shelf has appeared in the corner, slowly filling up with books. Helga continues to bloom.

"Are you really going to find a better apartment, like you said at the beginning?" I ask Mum.

"Do you know what?" Mum smiles. "I like it here. I think I'll stay. Even if the hot tap tries to sing a song of its people every time I go for a shower. I'm finally happy, James."

I want to give her a proper farewell and say *goodbye*, but I don't want her to get suspicious so, as I walk out the door, I say *see you* instead.

"A whole four days before I see you again." Mum sighs.

I don't know why that sentence feels so sad to me.

I swear I'm fine as I walk to school. I'm not nervous. Just ready. A bit excited, actually, like when you've packed your bags and are about to go on a trip.

Social Studies turns out to be more excellent than usual because out of nowhere, while the whole class is reading quietly, Roscoe bursts into tears.

Yes. The same boy who told me *boys don't cry*.

And not sitting at his desk with a tear trickling down his face, or a sob here and there. It's a loud howling, like the whole world is about to end. For once I'm disappointed not to be sitting somewhere with a good view.

But then I think about how it would feel if it was me,

and the way Mum whispers the word *compassion*, like it's heavier than the density of a neutron star, which is the heaviest known thing in the universe. She says it comes from Old French, meaning to "suffer with".

Miss Babette escorts Roscoe out of the class and is gone for a long time. When she comes back, it's without Roscoe and we don't see him for the rest of the day.

I don't see Yan at home time. I wait at the school gates until the last kid loitering around has gone. I walk home by myself, guessing Yan has Drama Club.

Isn't it funny how you can go up and down the same hill every day and think that's completely normal? Then suddenly you do the same thing with someone else and you can't imagine going back to how it was before.

I miss Yan. I miss seeing what strange book she's reading and not understanding half the stuff she says and the unique way she looks at the world. I like how we laughed in the car about a fart joke, how we lay in the field in one of Dad's memories, and how she gave me strawberry mochi when I cried that one time.

It's only been one week.

I don't know how I'll feel when I don't see her for good.

I kick at a rock and it rolls forwards and then starts rolling backwards.

Tonight is the last proper time I will spend with Dad before the mission. He interrogates me on what I want to do on the weekend, but I don't have the heart to tell him that it doesn't matter. Eventually, I settle on "hanging out and tinkering with Pop's motorcycle" so he'll leave me alone.

Dad decides on being adventurous in the kitchen and is roasting a whole chicken surrounded by sweet potatoes in the oven. What Dad didn't realize was that it would take hours to cook. In the meantime, we are starving *right now*. We eat Deconstructed Dessert while we wait because "who invented the order dinner should go in, anyway?" Dad questions.

I look down at the mug containing strawberry cheesecake, choc-chip ice cream, caramel sauce and crushed-up chocolate biscuits and I feel sad. Although this Dad is not that different from the Dad two weeks ago when he was still with Mum, he too is different in small ways that are big enough to count.

"Let's take a selfie," says Dad, holding up his phone.

"Why?" I ask. "It's not like this is a big moment or anything."

"Does it have to be?" asks Dad and snaps the photo.

We go to the Man Cave and I expect him to go straight to his computers. Or stand around with his hands on his hips, admiring Pop's motorcycle and pointing to bits and pieces and telling me what they are, as if I will magically need these facts in the future.

Instead, Dad goes over to his brass instruments and stares at them wistfully.

"Are you ever going to play these again?" I ask.

"I gave up when you were born. They're not exactly quiet. And your mum never liked the sound anyway."

"But Mum isn't here," I whisper.

Dad goes quiet.

I'm sure that was the wrong thing to say.

Dad picks up the trumpet and puts it to his mouth. The sound that comes out is a little shrill and pitchy, but he manages to play a tune.

"I've still got the chops!" he exclaims. "City Concert Hall, here I come!"

I leave Dad alone while he attempts to play a catchy advertising jingle and I crouch down on the living-room rug next to Tiger. She shows me her belly, which means she trusts me.

Now that I think about it, there are actually more things I'll miss in the present than I thought.

"You'll come with me on the mission, won't you?" I ask.

Tiger is noncommittal.

I read a story once about a time traveller who was able to carry, back to the past, a folded message inside their mouth. Tiger is only small. She'd only make a tiny ripple on the space–time continuum.

Dad and I eat dinner when it's supposed to be my bedtime and although I can't remember any of our conversations because we don't talk about anything important, I know it's spending time with each other that matters.

Launch day.

Dad has an important early meeting and is furiously doing a knot in his best tie. We both rush out the door at the same time.

"I'm going to miss you!" I blurt out before I realize what I'm saying.

"Wait. I'm seeing you tonight, right?" Dad asks, confused. "And I'm still having you this weekend?"

"Of course," I reply, ducking my head and walking faster. "See you."

I look back once and it upsets me to see Dad looking horrified because for a moment he thought his weekend with me might be taken away.

Yan's not in front of the house. She's not anywhere

227

along the footpath and she's nowhere on the other side, crashing into power poles and looking inside bushes. It makes no sense that I can't find her. I think back to when I first met Yan and how she said to me, "Everything has changed. Sometimes all it takes is one variable."

Roscoe's not in class. Miss Babette doesn't say anything about it, but the empty seat in front and to the left of me is glaringly obvious. I think about Roscoe at home, still bawling his eyes out. It should make me feel satisfied.

But it doesn't.

Before I begin to think I might be feeling sorry for Roscoe, I think instead about how he's going to be the same pain in the neck at any point of time, in any universe. For some reason, it's reassuring. Like the thought of Miss Babette, who hasn't changed one single bit in the past two weeks. And Principal Taylor, who Mum says was exactly the same when she was a kid and who's probably going to be exactly the same when we all grow up and send our kids to this school too.

* * *

I get a bit panicked when I walk up to the school gates after school because I haven't seen Yan since Wednesday. I panic that she's changed her mind about Mission Major Tom and is purposely avoiding me, even though there's no reason for her to be angry with me. Inside Dad's photo from 1997, she told me she *understood*.

I stand and I wait because I know she'll be here.

Because that's how things are going to end.

And I see her.

In the crowd, walking towards me, her eyes on the ground. She's not carrying a book. She stops next to me. Her eyes are still on the ground.

"Let's go," she says and starts walking again.

I hurry to catch up. "Are you angry with me?"

"No."

"Then why haven't I seen you for days?" I ask.

This just makes her walk faster. She can walk really fast without a book.

Even though my thighs are burning, I run as fast as I can up that hill to catch up with her.

"Tell me what you want me to do," I finally say. "To make it better. And I'll do it."

Yan stops and stares at me. "You really mean that?"

"Well," I say, "for the most part. But if it's something like take a one-way ticket to Mars, then I might have to think harder about it."

Yan looks like she's about to cry. Why is everyone I know crying?

"No one's...ever made me such a generous offer before," she says, sniffing. "It's made things worse!"

"What are you talking about?" I say.

"Are you really that clueless, James? I've been avoiding you because..." She puts her hands over her face. "I can't do this!"

"But you're the one who created Mission Major Tom –"

"James," says Yan. "This is not a logistical issue. Not everything is a logistical issue. I don't want to do it because I'll miss you!"

"Oh," I say.

I would not have guessed that. Never in a million years.

"But I will because of *altruism*," says Yan. "It comes from the Latin word meaning *to help others*. I will help you."

We've reached the House on the Hill. She doesn't run away. I find the key and we both enter with serious faces and serious hearts.

10 MINUTES UNTIL GO LAUNCH

We sit in the high-backed swivel chairs. The time machine sits between us. Yan has found a website on Dad's computer with an old-fashioned test countdown, the ones they used to play between programmes when colour TVs first came out and blew everyone's mind. We watch in silence as it fills up the whole screen, bright and flickery and rainbow striped.

Suddenly, I'm anxious, but I don't know why. Last-minute nerves, I guess. When I've had them in the past, Mum has told me to fight against them. She says it's what all brides are like before they get married and I'd always trusted her because it sounded like she was speaking from experience.

"Have you decided which one?" asks Yan, pushing the page of coordinates towards me.

I shake my head.

"This is the plan," says Yan. "I will drop you off at each one. Then, at the end, you tell me which one you decide on."

I nod.

"Let's get you ready," says Yan matter-of-factly.

Yan lifts up the silver helmet from the garage sale and holds it above my head.

"What is this for?" I ask. "I'm not going to take off on Pop's motorcycle, am I? Anyway, Dad hasn't finished putting the parts back, it doesn't even run yet."

"It's for drama," says Yan. "Just like the countdown. If you're going to go time travelling, you might as well make yourself believe you're going time travelling."

In my mind I hear Mum's voice echo the same message in different words, as she covered the cardboard boosters of the Rocket cake in foil.

"Even though it's not a real rocket, James, it helps with the illusion."

I let Yan put the helmet on me.

Tiger slinks into the room and puts her front paws up onto Yan's legs. Yan places the tiny, completed helmet onto Tiger's head. I'm surprised at how much Tiger looks like a legit space-age traveller. Yan opens the door of the motorcycle sidecar and gives me a sweeping bow. I smile at her through the plastic of the helmet visor.

I step into the sidecar, banging my knee on the door because I'm nervous. When I sit down on the vintage, black leather seat, it's like I'm a legit space-age traveller myself. I click on my seat belt. Tiger jumps in and stands on my shoulder, purring so loudly she sounds like a plane engine.

Yan is just like how I'd always imagined Major Tom's Ground Control in my head: surrounded by the flickering lights of the sixteen computers. She tethers the ethernet cable between her black box and Dad's computer.

Both time machines find each other. They connect.

The photo album opens. It shows the very last photo Dad took. The one of him and me from last night eating Deconstructed Dessert.

Yan looks down at the coordinates on the notepad and then back up at the countdown. I watch the countdown as well. The rainbow stripes all of a sudden blur into each other and I don't know why. Until I realize I might have a tear in my eye.

1 MINUTE UNTIL GO LAUNCH

"Commencing countdown," Yan says and gives me a thumbs up.

She turns the big button on the time machine and confirms the coordinates. I go to place my hands over my face because it's overwhelming, but they touch the plastic visor of my helmet. I tell myself I'm ready.

The album starts flicking back through photos so fast it's almost like my life is counting backwards. It slows down and stops and on the screen is a photo of me. Aged seven. In my NASA space pyjamas. Pouting because I didn't want to smile for the camera like Dad told me.

I want to ask Yan how the computer monitors in the room have all turned themselves on and are counting down too.

"Good luck, Major James," says Yan.

The lights flicker. There's a low humming in the air. Time s l o w s and thick white smoke covers the floor and floats upwards towards me. I squeeze my eyes shut.

10

9

8

7

6

5

4

3

2

1

WE HAVE LIFT-OFF

04:129:23:00

I open my eyes. I'm seven years old. *Whoa.* I have gone a long way back in time. Snuggled in my bed – with Tiger at my feet and my night-light that is a globe next to me – everything should be safe. But I'm filled with a fear so intense it presses against all my insides. Too big for my small body, it threatens to blow up my heart.

Dad comes into the room, and I'm surprised at how young he is. He looks like a stranger. His hair actually has a colour. But when he sits close to me on the bed and starts comforting me, I know it's definitely Dad. He tells me that everything's going to be okay. That Major Tom died painlessly in space. Like going to sleep.

Mum is at the door and she's different too. I'm not sure if I can get used to my parents looking this young. She tells me that Major Tom didn't die, that the song is about him choosing to disconnect from earth.

A warm, sweet feeling like dessert begins to dissolve the fear in my belly. The whole world is okay. Both of my parents are working together to make it all better. I like being seven years old again; being protected, feeling safe.

But hang on.

Seven-year-old me didn't realize, or has since forgotten, that each of his parents is telling him a completely different story.

Something isn't quite right.

Both my parents abruptly leave the room.

I guess this is the part where I snuggle down under the covers and fall asleep.

Tiger jumps off the bed and looks at me. I shake my head, and she stares intently at me out of her space helmet. I get out from under the covers and follow her. I creep towards the door and peek through the gap.

"Why did you tell him Major Tom *dies*?" Mum hisses to Dad angrily.

"Because I'm being truthful," Dad answers back just as angrily.

"You know he's not equipped to deal with that topic yet!"

"Well, he has to learn about life and death eventually. You can't treat him like a little boy for ever."

Mum walks off.

"I can't believe you're picking a fight over an imaginary character!" Dad shouts down the hall.

"He's not just an imaginary character, he's Major Tom!" Mum shouts back.

I stare in shock. This is not how I remembered this moment.

"Ground Control, can you hear me?" I whisper. "We are terminating this destination. Please program in the next coordinates."

00:250:05:00

I'm relieved when I find myself at my eleventh birthday party. The huge space-scape cake is exactly how I remembered it: the bumpy surface of an unknown planet with a spaceship on it, aliens peeking out of the craters. Maybe it's not scientifically accurate and real aliens wouldn't really look like that because they would most likely be forms of bacteria...but all of it is made out of edible royal icing and I love it.

But no one from school is saying how awesome it is because... No one has showed up for my party. Not even Roscoe. And I'm... Shattered.

I don't remember this bit at all. The *feeling so disappointed* bit.

Did I block it out? Or have I remembered incorrectly? All I honestly can recollect is the cake and the food. And there *is* a mountain of food, exactly how it looked in my head, because my parents catered for twenty people.

Cousins Jackson and Harry are bouncing madly on the trampoline. I remember that I go and join them at this point, before the eating starts.

Tiger is sitting on the lawn twitching her tail. She goes to lick the side of her body but is restricted by her space helmet.

I see her look up at me and wink. When she bounces off, I follow.

Strangely, I find my parents behind the garden shed, where all the empty plastic flowerpots and extra mulch are piled up. I approach slowly, with my weightless space-traveller walk, so they don't hear me.

"I can't believe I trusted you with the invitations and you messed it up!" Mum exclaims.

Oh.

Maybe I'm not the least popular kid in the class after all. Did Dad just forget to organize it?

"Honest mistakes happen," replies Dad and makes a face. "But I'm not the one who decided to continue the charade and pretend twenty kids were still coming!"

It's Mum's turn to make a face.

I want to tell both of them *time out*.

I can take all the food to school on Monday and have a celebration there. Mrs Tagliatelle will know what to do. I wonder if we can even use the staffroom...

Instead, my parents do this *adult thing* where they bring up something else for absolutely no reason other than they like to keep arguing.

"I thought you were going to bake the cake," Dad complains.

"I...ran out of time," replies Mum, wriggling uncomfortably with her answer. "But I ordered the best cake I could. It's awesome, no?"

It is awesome, Mum, I want to confirm.

"That's not the point," Dad replies. "You've told him every single year that you'll bake the cake. And you never have."

Mum has already explained to me how Ah Ma never baked her a cake from *The Australian Women's Weekly Children's Birthday Cake Book* and that, in turn, is why it's hard for her to do so too. That it's about more than pouring batter into a tin and then icing the cake that comes out. That it's about breaking behaviours and changing yourself.

I want to shout to her that *I understand*.

I watch as Dad's words collide into Mum like an asteroid. Mum's cheeks turn pink, but she doesn't cry.

"Then why don't *you* bake the cake!" Mum shouts. "You've never even offered!"

Dad puts his finger to his lips and motions towards the trampoline. Mum claps her hand across her mouth.

I don't want to hear any more. I pull away and flatten myself against the shed. My eleventh birthday party had an awesome cake, but the rest of it wasn't awesome at all. On the inside, I guess I always knew.

"Major James to Ground Control. Please stand by with the next coordinates."

I lean my head back on the shed and put my hands over my face, but they touch the plastic helmet visor instead.

00:360:00:20

When I take my hands off the plastic visor, I'm in the same eleven-year-old body, but I'm on fire. Not only are my thighs burning, I'm burning all over. I'm trailing behind Mum, with Dad behind me, and we're hiking Reabold Hill because Mrs Stonecutter told us it'd be a fun family activity.

Mum stops. She's puffing and sweating, and her face is all red. She pulls out a bottle of water and hands it to me first.

I take it gratefully.

I know we all recall it as funny when we went up Reabold Hill. Only it hurts way more than I remember.

But I tell myself that once we reach the top and take that beautiful sunset photo of the three of us, it'll be worth it. The photo that Mum will share on social media and that will get hundreds of likes and comments, such as "Perfect!", "Well done the three of you" and "Hitting family goals".

Tiger is running on up ahead and I force myself to pump my legs a little harder.

There's the sound of rocks falling followed by an "Ouch" and I turn around to see Dad has tripped and hurt his ankle. It's bleeding.

Oh. I totally forgot about this part.

"Pass us a plaster, will you?" Dad says to Mum.

"I don't have any plasters," replies Mum.

"Why didn't you bring any plasters?" Dad sounds overly angry.

"Kimberley told me it's an easy trail. I didn't think

anyone would get hurt." Mum sounds overly emotional.

I don't remember this. Or do I? Before I know it, Mum is crying even though it's Dad who's sitting on the ground with a bleeding ankle. There's still at least half an hour till we reach the top and I can't stand to be here one more second.

I feel bad for both my parents. They seem miserable, even though this is supposed to be a fun family activity. And it's not really Mrs Stonecutter's fault that we're all lousy outdoors people and Dad tripped. I wish I knew what to do. What to say to make the situation okay.

But I don't remember doing or saying anything. I guess I froze and pretended to be invisible and kept hiking and wishing my parents weren't fighting.

I remember something else now: around this time my parents fought *all* the time. Not only on this hike up Reabold Hill. Over other stuff too, not just plasters.

I tell the Old Me, the one who has to keep going, that everything will be perfect at the top. For a little while anyway. For a bubble in time we will have the sunset behind us and Dad's long selfie arm and a perfect snapshot. But bubbles are formed when the surface tension between water and air weakens. It is a momentary thing before the

244

water and air go back to being strong and independent of each other.

I want to tell him that things will only get better for good once his parents decide to go their separate ways. Only then will they stop fighting and become happier as two separate and individual people.

"Are you there, Ground Control?" I say shakily. "Please proceed with the next coordinates."

00:360:05:45

My whole body stops hurting. The thirst and the onset of sunburn goes away. It's last winter and it's raining outside. I'm protected underneath a sheet fort that smells like the eucalyptus washing powder that Mum always uses. It's fresh and comforting. Tiger stretches out her front paw, opens up a hole in the sheets and disappears.

It is peaceful. Wonderful. *Plain old nostalgic.* I'm staring into space through a tiny tear in the fabric, not doing anything, when Dad slides in next to me.

I know how this part goes.

I ask him, "What are you doing?"

And he replies, "Hiding from your mum."

Instead of thinking that Dad is making one of his awful Dad Jokes, I go off script and ask, "What's wrong?"

Dad goes quiet. "A lot of things," he finally says. "But they're not for you to worry about."

Which is the worst response because, of course, I start worrying now that he's brought it into existence.

The sheets rustle. Mum crawls into the fort on my other side and lies down.

"How are you, Mum?" I ask. I put my hand in the crook of her arm.

"I don't know," replies Mum and lets out a sigh. "I honestly don't know."

The three of us lie there. I had remembered this moment as being cosy and calm, lying there in each other's company and listening to the rain outside, not needing to talk.

But I can see the situation for what it is now.

I can feel Mum's pain. I can feel Dad's pain. And I'm hurting too.

I'd rather take the whole-body pain of Reabold Hill than this.

I want to fade away.

"Ground Control," I whisper. "You know the drill."

00:347:21:06

The giant popcorn and Coke appear in my arms so suddenly I almost drop them.

I glitch in and out for a little bit.

Dad is checking the time on his phone. In my memories, I'm sure he was checking it on his watch. Also, in my memories I have a bag of chocolate Fantales, but they are nowhere to be seen. I shuffle as close to him as my full arms will let me.

"Happy birthday, Dad!" I blurt out. "I'm glad we're here to see your favourite movie from when you were a kid. I'm going to do my best to love this movie."

Dad is genuinely surprised. His face softens and his eyes crinkle at the corners.

"I haven't watched this movie for decades...it's probably pretty lame now, to be honest! I just want you to be part of a happy memory I once had."

Dad sounds so determined, like he can take his happiness from the past and transfer it directly to me, like a computer downloads content onto a drive. I wish it was that easy too.

He turns back to his phone. He's furiously texting.

I can't help having that awful sensation when you're waiting and waiting for someone and they're nowhere to be seen, although you know you can trust them to arrive on time. Even though I already know how this scene ends. Mum will walk in four minutes before the movie starts.

And here she is.

Mum rushes in, still in her work clothes and smelling like the train. I get ready to step through the open door of the cinema.

Except Mum motions to Dad and they both go to a corner.

Do I remember this?

Oh, of course I do.

I just chose to block it from my memory.

Original me will edge closer to the cinema to give his parents the clue it's time to go in, as that's all he can do. But this future, emboldened version of me diverges and inches closer to my parents.

They have an argument that goes for three minutes.

At first, it's about Mum's tardiness, then it quickly morphs out of control and becomes an ugly, stumbling, lopsided lava monster that fans the flames of Mum's hotheadedness. That flips open Dad's head, taking out the logic and replacing it with rocks.

Even the ticket attendant starts to look uncomfortable. Tiger, sitting on the counter with her space helmet, wearing an attendant's bow tie and waistcoat, flicks her tail disapprovingly.

I speak to Yan and ask her to take me away. The giant Coke is freezing my hand and the buttered popcorn – which is the most delicious smell in the world – is making me sick.

Are you listening, Ground Control?

00:249:22:22

This is the last set of coordinates.

I've been able to keep track of time, although my head is spinning. Maybe because I'm sitting in the revolving restaurant as it slowly clicks and chugs along, the grand pianist playing something that sounds like it's for a funeral. Tiger shares the piano bench and contributes by lowering a paw onto an ominous key.

I slide my hands, still tingling from the cold Coke, up the front of my good shirt and I adjust my clip-on bow tie.

Mum, sitting next to me, stops staring at her glass of water and smiles at me.

Mum looks...

Thin.

I remember she went on a ridiculous juice diet to fit into her high school ball dress, but we thought it was one of her passing phases, like Reabold Hill, and ignored it. I guess she had faded so gradually in front of our eyes we never saw her disappear.

I stand up abruptly because I know what's going to happen next. Even though I can hear Yan's words in my head telling me I shouldn't interfere, I need to stop Mrs Stonecutter from punching that wine glass out of the air and spoiling Mum's dress.

The wine glass is already making its trajectory.

I make my move and rush in front of Mrs Stonecutter.

"No! James!"

Is that Mum? It's not Mum's voice.

Mrs Stonecutter hands her baby over to her husband and I feel her arms close upon me and she spins me around one-eighty degrees. Mrs Stonecutter goes "ouch". The wine glass hits her in the back.

The same wine glass that would have hit me in the head.

That would have hit Mum in the face if it had continued on its original path.

Oh.

"Thank you," whispers Mum, trembling all over in that tiny wisp of a dress as I go over to her and she takes me in her arms and strokes my hair.

I stare awestruck at Mrs Stonecutter, who is rubbing her back and wiping wine off her expensive sparkly dress.

Why would she do something like that when she's a villain?

The person who lost control of their wine apologizes profusely to Mrs Stonecutter.

"You could have seriously hurt someone," Mrs Stonecutter shouts. She glares at the room as though everybody owes her an answer. "I'm a lawyer, by the way. Unless you want to end up as a witness in court, I'd go back to eating!"

Mum sits there stunned, a tiny spot of wine on her dress.

"Oh, Sophie! Come with me, let's go fix ourselves up," says Mrs Stonecutter and they hastily flee.

I look down and there is a spot of wine on me too.

I hurry off after them.

"James!" Dad shouts, but I don't turn to see if he comes after me.

Tiger plays another ominous note.

Mum and Mrs Stonecutter go into the unisex toilet together. I press my ear against the door. Not that I need to because Mrs Stonecutter is always talking loudly, like she's in court defending another sorry criminal.

"Firstly, you look terrible. You need to start eating," she says. "Secondly, I have never seen you look so miserable. It's time to do something about it. You know that the love story is well and truly *over*."

Mum mumbles something. I don't catch it because she's using her soft voice.

"I can help you," Mrs Stonecutter says in a kinder voice. "I know lots of excellent family lawyers. Now, let's dry that face of yours. There, there."

There is the sound of paper towels being pulled out of the dispenser and a nose being blown.

Static crackles in my ear. I hear Yan's voice, loud and clear, for the first time since I started the journey.

"Major James, please confirm your final coordinates. I wish to remind you that your choice is permanent. Choose wisely."

My answer is swift. "None."

Silence.

"What do you mean *none*?" exclaims Yan, forgetting to use her serious Ground Control voice.

I don't want to be part of a world where my parents fight over things like a song about a pretend spaceman. Where they have to take their arguments behind the shed so that I don't hear. Where they might end up holding hands under the table of a revolving restaurant because they think about the times when they used to love each other, but they don't love each other any more.

But these things are only memories. And the good thing about memories is that you can leave them behind where they belong.

"I don't want to live in the past any more."

Silence.

"Please confirm that the mission is terminated."

"The mission is terminated," I repeat. "Bring me home, Ground Control."

+ 0 DAYS 0 HOURS
0 MINUTES 18 SECONDS

Man Cave. Pop's silver motorcycle. Tiger on my knee. Sixteen blinking computers.

Everything looks the same. But everything has changed.

The countdown screens all read *0*. The white smoke on the ground is clearing. Time moves at normal speed.

Shakily, I get out of the sidecar and approach Yan. Her back is to me as she sits at the computer desk. She is typing furiously on the keyboard and clicking on the mouse.

On the screen, tabs are opening by themselves. Charts. Graphs. A beating heart. A pulse. A blueprint of Pop's motorcycle. A wedding photo. An X-ray of Tiger. A photo of me as a baby. A video of the entire galaxy revolving.

"I can't get these two time machines to separate," exclaims Yan. "They seem to have grown somewhat... attached to each other."

The final thing I hear are her panicked words instructing me to, "Hold on to your helmet! It looks like we're about to— "

I'm sitting on the couch next to Yan, with Tiger between us. There's a retro kids movie playing on the TV that I've never seen before. Suddenly it ends and the credits play. Yan is dabbing her eyes with a tissue but she looks like she's been crying and hiccupping for longer than that.

"What on earth is going –" I start to say, but right then Dad delivers two Deconstructed Desserts and I gratefully take one because, well, time travelling is a hungry business.

Baked pavlova meringue, cream, raspberries, blueberries, smashed-up chocolate biscuits and crushed honeycomb bars. I go to put a big spoonful in my mouth. It hits the plastic shield of my helmet.

"How do I make this thing stop?" says Yan as she

shakes her black box and holds it up to her ear. "Serves me right for using those cheap bits when I built this thing! Oh no! Here we go—"

I slam the brakes on my scooter.

Yan goes whizzing past on hers and shouts, "I win!"

"Says who?" I shout back.

"Says us," replies Yan as she slows down ahead of me and points. "You see that Norfolk pine back there? We agreed we'd race from there up to this lamp post."

I reach out and touch the lamp post. It feels solid and real. Even then I feel tempted to feel all the way around it just to make sure.

Yan takes the time machine out of her backpack and examines it. "Don't panic. I'm still working on it."

"I wasn't even aware your time machine could go forward in time!"

"Well, it is a *time machine*," answers Yan haughtily.

"Are we having fun?" Mum asks as she catches up and slows her scooter down.

Yan nods enthusiastically, her cheeks flushed and pink.

"You should hear about the first time we did this." Mum laughs. "It was pouring with rain and I made James wear this giant yellow raincoat twice as big as his body!"

My hands go up to my cheeks 'cos I think they're turning pink too, but they slap against my helmet.

"It's getting dark," says Mum. "How about we head back and get hot chocolate?"

"Yes please," replies Yan.

I stare at the perfect blue sky, turning orange at the edges, and I get ready to spin my scooter around.

"Uh-oh," says Yan.

"Oh no, not again," I reply.

"Hang on, I—"

I feel myself tipping sideways into the sky.

The ground seems a long way down from the bar stool I'm seated on. I'm in a house I haven't seen before. I look around at the unfamiliar kitchen and the old, chipped laminate on the breakfast bar. Beside me, Yan kicks her legs in anticipation. Mrs Chen places a huge plate of steamed dumplings in front of us. I apologize to her that I don't use chopsticks very well. She passes me a fork without making me feel embarrassed.

"I *can* fix it," says Yan. She gives the time machine a loud thump.

"What happens if we don't land back in the present?" I ask, suddenly scared.

"We will," replies Yan firmly.

I stab a dumpling and go to put it in my mouth, but Yan says, "Dip it into the soy sauce first and then into the cut chillies – they're fresh from our front yard. Look, like this."

I remember to take my helmet off first.

I follow her directions and then almost choke. The chillies are *spicy*. But delicious.

"You'll get used to it in time," says Yan, unfazed.

I know that in time I'll also not think it's strange that the vegetable garden is at the front of the house (it's also at the back) and I'll understand why Mrs Chen thinks harm might come to Yan if she walks home alone down an unknown route.

Mrs Chen has placed a saucer of milk on the kitchen floor for Tiger, who is also having a new experience. Mum never lets her have milk for good reason – Tiger is lactose intolerant, and it's not only Tiger who will regret it later. But for the time being, she's living for the moment.

The light above us flickers.

We both hold hands.

"Hold on tight!" shouts Yan and then...

My feet touch solid ground.

"Welcome home," says Yan.

The first thing I do is give her a big hug.

She stands very still as I awkwardly squeeze her.

"What's wrong?" I ask.

"I don't come from a family of huggers, shall we say," she replies.

"Oh. I guess there's still a lot I need to learn about you."

"But if you promise to hug me once in a while, then I can learn how to do it properly," she says to me almost shyly.

"Of course," I say and finally look around. "What happened?"

"It appears we encountered a technical problem,"

replies Yan. "While I was trying to bring you back to the present, the time machine started to glitch. Thank all the Major Toms, I finally managed to land you! We might have lost a few days." She scrunches up her face. "Don't get upset now. Oh, my goodness, look at this! Isn't it the cutest?"

We're standing behind a long trestle table covered in a white linen cloth. Right in front of us is a Cuddly Koala cake, covered in chocolate icing, the butter cake paws holding onto a branch made of liquorice and mint leaf lollies.

We're in the school auditorium.

On the day of the cake competition.

I see Tiger sitting very still on top of the plastic chairs stacked in the corner, far away from the cakes. Maybe she's worried she might get mistaken for one.

Yan points and giggles. It's a Friendly Ghost cake, made exactly like in the official *Australian Women's Weekly Children's Birthday Cake Book*. I never understood – even after exhausting all the scientific and philosophical reasons – why the eyes are made out of two real eggshells.

She swoons at the Typewriter cake with the smartie keys and a real message sitting inside the roller that reads,

You must have been warned against letting the golden hours slip by; but some of them are golden only because we let them slip by. – James M. Barrie

It's noisy in here because all of a sudden, every parent who has paid their five-dollar entry fee is a professional cake critic. I look down at all the labels I had helped Mrs Tagliatelle make. The borders are definitely made of slices of cake and have not changed. The big clock above the stage at the front reveals that there are ten minutes remaining before the winners are announced.

"Mum!" I say and I scan the room full of people. I see her to the right, near the red stage curtain.

I grab hold of Yan's hand and we slowly weave past the tables full of cakes and the parents pondering them so seriously.

"Mum!"

She stops talking and the person who she's speaking to turns around.

It's Mrs Stonecutter. She's done something different to her hair. It's a completely different colour. And all miserable in the corner is Roscoe.

"I want to say good luck, Mum. I don't care who wins. Yours is the best cake in my opinion... Ahh, where's the cake, by the way?"

She seems confused. "Thanks, James. That's so kind of you. I thought you were just looking at it a moment ago?"

"Here," says Yan, dragging me away.

Mum has nailed the vintage duck-egg blue colour. She's edged the whole stove in silver sugar balls. The plates and cups rest along the top, with the pot and pan sitting on burners of coiled liquorice. Simmering away are fried eggs crafted out of white marshmallow and yellow Smarties, and tomatoes made of orange-shelled chocolate balls. A little dishcloth made from a fruit strap hangs over a liquorice oven handle. It's a beauty. My eyes mist up.

Next to it, towering three times as tall, is Mrs Stonecutter's Rocket cake. I'd secretly hoped the cake would have turned out to be a disaster because Mrs Stonecutter is a villain and villains are supposed to fail.

But the Rocket cake is actually quite good.

I guess because Mrs Stonecutter is not a true villain after all. Not that I would call her a hero. An *anti-hero* at a stretch.

I like how she's iced it white, like a real rocket should be, and decorated it very simply with red lolly accents.

"Mum wanted to make it rainbow colours, but I talked

her out of it," Roscoe grumbles, appearing at the table with his hands in his pockets.

"When are you coming back to school?" I ask.

"Huh? I was at school today. You spent all day shooting dirty looks at me, like you normally do, remember? Dude, every time I make a sound you seem to think it's about you. I mean, sometimes it is. But not always."

"Oh." I guess I'm still stuck in Friday when it's actually next Tuesday now.

Call it a case of time traveller's jet lag.

"I hope you're okay," I say to Roscoe, despite what I think of him.

"I'm all right," Roscoe replies, looking at me with raised eyebrows. "I'll be better when my dad decides to come back home. It's been a whole week."

"What happened to your dad?"

Not that I *care* or anything.

The sound of speaker feedback cuts through the auditorium and everyone stops talking and faces the front. On the stage, Principal Taylor fumbles with the microphone. Mrs Tagliatelle and Ms Page stand there awkwardly.

"Welcome to our annual Summerlake Primary School Cake Competition."

There is a small smatter of applause.

"Dad ran off to Magnetic Island with our tax accountant," Roscoe whispers. "Mum reckons it's because she's not special. Because songs are written for girls called Sara but not for ones called Kimberley. She won't listen when I say I think she's super."

Oh. I feel bad for Roscoe. I couldn't imagine Dad doing something like that.

"I'm sorry to hear that," I whisper back.

"I'm proud of the two of you having this mature conversation, but shush," says Yan. "They're about to announce the winner."

"Who are you?" says Roscoe.

"I'm Yan," she replies, as if he ought to know.

Principal Taylor grapples nervously with the envelope. "And the winner is..."

"Stove cake," I whisper under my breath.

"Rocket cake," Roscoe whispers under his.

"Tip Truck," Yan randomly whispers.

"...Tip Truck!" roars Principal Taylor.

"For the first time in the history of this competition, a tip truck has been entered with a fully functioning rear tray," continues Principal Taylor. "The judges applaud this incredible feat of engineering."

Everyone claps politely. There are some sad groans of defeat. Somewhere in the back, someone yells, "Rigged!" I look over and it's the man in the golf gear.

The winner, a delighted grandfather, gets up onstage and bows solemnly as Principal Taylor places the winner's golden apron over his head. Everyone claps again.

"I still think your cake is the best," I say, turning to Mum.

"Thank you, treasure," she replies. "Make sure you tell Dad the same thing about his cake."

"*His* cake?"

+ 4 DAYS 23 HOURS 04 MINUTES

"Don't act like you've forgotten," says Mum and she points. "Over there."

Across the room, Dad sticks up his hand and offers a small, awkward wave.

"When has Dad ever baked? He doesn't even have cake tins..."

Yan gives me a nudge and a mysterious look.

"Oh!"

Dad offers another small wave and this time I'm wading through the crowd.

"This is another one of your secret plans, isn't it?" I ask Yan.

"Well, I couldn't let a perfectly good set of tins that someone so kindly gifted me go to waste, could I?"

* * *

Dad gives me this strange, self-conscious sideways hug as we look down at the cake in front of us. Not quite symmetrical and not quite uniform – even though it's made by someone who prides themselves on precise dimensions – sits the White Rabbit. It also looks like it might have shed half of its desiccated coconut fur on the journey here. But what it lacks in all those areas it makes up for with a skilfully made pink smartie nose that some will of the universe seems to have split perfectly in half.

Dad hasn't attempted to dye the desiccated coconut pink to make the insides of the ears, but...

"It's a winner to me," I say.

Dad turns red and pushes his glasses back up.

"There's my mum! I told her to come and see all the pretty cakes," Yan suddenly exclaims.

I see a bewildered lady slowly edging though the auditorium door, clutching her purse.

"I said she'd like it and maybe she could even enter one day!" continues Yan with enthusiasm. "That the community will welcome her."

Mrs Chen makes a disapproving face. She sees Yan

and heads in our direction.

Yan says something excitedly to her mum in Chinese. But her mother replies in a stern tone and I watch as Yan's shoulders slump, as she withdraws into herself.

Strangely, although she has just got here, Mrs Chen appears to be in a rush to leave. Yan nods in silence and I wonder where the determined and bold girl I know has gone. She gets her backpack ready to go.

I feel a hand on my head. I turn around and I expect it to be Dad.

It's Mum.

She goes up to Mrs Chen and starts speaking to her in Chinese. Mum takes her over to the Stove cake. Points to the Rocket cake and stretches out the length of her arms. Both of them laugh.

I turn to Yan, who stares at Mum in amazement.

"There are activists, Nobel prize winners and people changing the planet whom I greatly admire," says Yan quietly. "But *that's* who I want to be when I grow up."

Once again, Yan makes me see things through different eyes.

So that now I, too, believe I have X-ray eyes.

Mrs Chen inspects a few more cakes, then speaks to

Yan. Mrs Chen turns to give me a guarded smile, then leaves by herself.

"The future might take a while," Yan says. "But at least Ma Ma says I can stay till the end."

"Well, we have all the time in the world," I say.

Yan beams.

"Excuse me, everyone!"

Back up on the stage, Mrs Tagliatelle takes the microphone off Principal Taylor.

"Another historical first is about to occur. The judges have decided that this year, in order to bring a bit of fun back into the competition..."

I swear she's making eye contact with all the adults.

"...we're going to have a Public Choice Award. Based on *taste*."

Teachers start coming out of the shadows with cake knives. Next to us, I watch as the Tip Truck, with its fully functioning rear tray, gets reduced to slices and corners of mush. Across the room, two teachers tilt the Rocket cake on its side and cut through it like it's a rack of lamb.

Another teacher starts taking the little doll's plates, cups, pot and pan off Mum's cake.

Pieces of cake are placed on labelled plates and passed around.

I get a piece of Dolly Varden and Yan gets a piece of the Smiley Shark. I watch as Dad sniffs his piece of Timothy Tiger and then tries a mouthful.

The next plate that gets passed to me is a piece of the Candy Castle.

I look across the room and I see the dad who came in that day two weeks ago and asked me which cake he should pick. I don't recognize him at first because he's wearing casual clothes instead of that sharp suit, and he doesn't have his phone glued to his ear. Instead he's talking and laughing with his family.

I see he took my advice to use Skittles instead of Smarties.

I smile.

The dad notices me. Recognition passes over his face and he waves.

I wave back.

The room surges and switches as everyone beelines for the slices of cake they want to sample. I end up tasting a bit of both Mum and Dad's creations, but I can't decide which to vote for. The Stove cake tastes like one you'd get from a professional bakery and I think of all the evenings Mum has spent getting it right. The White Rabbit, though, has a taste that is different from every other. It has a delicious secret ingredient that Dad has either scientifically and deliberately concocted or (most likely) accidentally added in.

That's when I have a sudden and unexpected revelation. Like the universe is lifting up a corner so that I can see the answer. That Mum, sweet and nostalgic, is just like her cake, and that Dad, chaotic and creative, is just like his. That I can love both of them at the same time because life is not a competition with only one winner. That I can fit in the centre where two circles overlap.

+ 4 DAYS 23 HOURS 49 MINUTES

The Public Choice voting poll is located on the stage with Mrs Tagliatelle.

I already knew about this *plot twist*, being a valued member of the Cake Committee, of course, but I didn't want to spoil the *plot twist* by saying anything before.

I've decided I'm going to vote for the dad who everyone made fun of on social media, but who has bravely decided to replicate his Echidna Ice-cream Cake for the competition. If it's possible, it looks even worse the second time around because when the cake started melting, the features of the face began to move in different directions.

But if we're talking about taste alone, a chocolate ice cream and chocolate-covered biscuit combo cannot be beaten.

"Do you think this historical first has brought some fun back into the competition?" I ask Mrs Tagliatelle as I slip my vote into the box.

"Pet!" she exclaims. "Like an overbaked cake, this competition is too far gone! It's given me nothing but stress this year. I honestly hope they'll cancel it!"

What happened next is the stuff of school legend.

It would have been easy to blame it on Yan. After all, it's possible she's an actual time traveller. Who could have – at the very least – if not stopped it, given a clue or a warning. But didn't.

The most popular theory blames it on Principal Taylor, since the Summerlake Primary School Cake Competition was put "on hiatus" (although not strictly "cancelled") afterwards and has been on hiatus since.

But if you ask me, I swear it was the man in the golf gear. If I remember correctly, as I headed off the stage, I saw him being handed a piece of cake like everyone else. I saw him stare at the name of the cake on the paper plate.

Then he threw the cake onto the floor.

The cake splattered upwards onto the grandparent

who had won the golden apron for his Tip Truck.

But who knows if I'm right, because if there's one thing I've learned, it's that you can't always trust a memory, can you?

All of a sudden, people are *throwing cake at each other*. But why would there be a cake fight at a cake baking competition?

A lump of cake smacks me in the side of my head.

I look over at Yan and she already has icing stuck in her hair, along with jelly babies and bits of pink musk stick. I watch as she hesitantly plunges her hand into the remains of the Farmyard cake, forms a firm ball and aims it at me.

Suddenly there is cake, ice cream and jelly flying everywhere and I'm flinging handfuls of it as fast and hard as I can too.

At Dad. At Mum. At Roscoe and at Mrs Stonecutter.

"This is too crazy for a *plot twist*, don't you think?" I yell out to Yan above the noise.

"But are you enjoying yourself?"

"Yes."

"Then everything in the past needed to happen in order to lead to this very moment in time. It is a simple and scientific cause and effect!" Yan shouts back.

She stops and smiles. "Or you can just live in the moment and not question it too much!"

I'm laughing. She's laughing. We go sliding down onto the floorboards.

"Are you sure you're definitely staying?" Yan asks as we both stare at each other.

"Definitely," I say. "I understand now. I can't go back. I don't want to go back."

"Does it still hurt, being in the present?"

"It'll always hurt."

"That's why you need a friend, James Greenaway."

I try to stand up and I offer Yan my hand, but we both go sliding down again.

It takes us a few goes, in which I begin to feel we've been transported into a quaint old-fashioned book about a land of lollies, where the characters ice skate on buttercream.

Yan wipes icing off her nose, goes quiet and stares past my shoulder.

I turn around and standing there is Roscoe Stonecutter.

He throws a handful of cake at me and it splats weakly on my shoulder. I look at it slide down my arm and I'm trying to figure out what cake it is, but every cake at this point is the same smooshed-up vanilla batter and supermarket lolly crumbed chaos; they have become one with the cake universe.

I stare at Roscoe and he stares at me.

"Is that the best you can do?" I say.

I hurl a cake ball at him, and it hits him right in the centre of his chest.

Roscoe stares down at his designer shirt, which is already ruined anyway. Then he starts to laugh.

And I'm laughing too.

"Hey, do you think if I have a birthday party this year you'd come?" I ask carefully.

"If I get an invite," mumbles Roscoe.

I'll make sure Dad is not in charge of the invitations this time.

"Birthday party?" Yan pipes up. "Never in my eleven years have I ever been to one! What date in the future should I expect my invite?"

* * *

We find out the next day that the winner of the Public Choice Award is the Choo-Choo Train.

In the end, it wasn't technical execution, difficulty level, popularity, cake bias or anything like that at all. The Choo-Choo Train won because, with its impressive four carriages, it had the most lollies.

00:000:00:01

"So," says Mum, looking at me and Dad, as we stand in the school car park.

I guess she's trying to figure out who looks worse.

Over to the side, Mrs Tagliatelle is blasting people down with the fire hose.

"So," says Dad.

I think when covered in cake everyone looks the same.

Equally bad.

"Hungry?" asks Mum.

Dad's stomach makes a growling noise. "What are you suggesting?"

"Maybe we can grab a pizza for dinner. Kimberley Stonecutter suggested this new place that's opened up down the road. Apparently, their potato and pesto pizza is to die for."

Dad groans.

"Is this anything like that nouvelle cuisine place she suggested for your birthday?"

But Dad has not run off in horror and is walking alongside with Mum as she leads the way.

"They have a meat-lovers house special."

"Now you've got my attention," says Dad.

I believe when adults have this sort of easy conversation, it's because they have something together called *history*.

"Meow," says Tiger.

"Oh." Mum picks her up. "How on earth did you get here?"

Tiger purrs.

"We'd better dine al fresco then," says Mum. "Guess it's a nice night for it."

Dad doesn't disagree.

I walk between my parents and dodge the cracks in the pavement. I don't pressure myself that this moment needs to become a new favourite memory to replace my old ones.

I just enjoy myself in the moment, because I finally understand that it's the one place where everyone truly belongs at any one point in time.

SHIRLEY MARR is a first-generation Chinese-Australian author living in sunny Perth. Shirley describes herself as having a Western mind and an Eastern heart and likes to write in the space in the middle where both collide, basing her stories on her own personal experiences of migration and growing up.

Arriving in mainland Australia from Christmas Island as a seven-year-old in the 1980s and experiencing the good, the bad and the wonder that comes with culture shock, Shirley has been in love with reading and writing from that early age.

Her debut novel, *A Glasshouse of Stars*, was the winner of the Children's Book Council of Australia Younger Readers Book of the Year award.

ACKNOWLEDGEMENTS

Thank you to my dear friend H. M. Waugh, whose unfortunate childhood memory of "Space Oddity" became the inspiration for James's own! To my amazing agent Gemma Cooper, who I am forever indebted to; to Zoe Walton, who did actually bake the most amazing Ginger Neville cake, and to Krista Vitola, Mary Verney and Rebecca Hill, who are the most incredible women to work with. To the hardworking and supportive teams at Penguin Random House Australia, Simon & Schuster US and Usborne Books UK. To everyone who has supported and encouraged me, who dragged me out to share chai lattes, cake and pizza – thank you for keeping me sane. To the iconic *Australian Women's Weekly Children's Birthday Cake Book*, which inspired the baking competition in this story, with apologies that I've fictionalized a cake name or two along the way. Finally, thank you to all my readers, you allow me to do what I do and that is all I can ever ask for.

Look out for these other titles from master storyteller, SHIRLEY MARR:

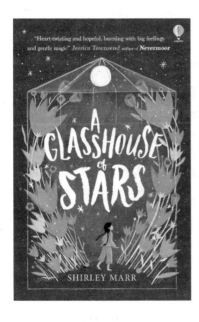

"*Heart-twisting and hopeful, bursting with big feelings and gentle magic.*"
Jessica Townsend

"*Gentle yet powerful, truly a book to treasure.*"
Sophie Anderson

USBORNE QUICKLINKS

In this story, the parents who enter the cake competition
follow cake decorating recipes from *The Australian
Women's Weekly's Children's Birthday Cake Book*. It was
first published in 1980 and sold more than half
a million copies.

Scan the code for links to websites where you can see
cakes from *The Australian Women's Weekly Birthday Cake
Book* and find tips and inspiration for decorating your
own cakes, or go to usborne.com/Quicklinks and type
in the title of this book.

.

Children should be supervised online. Please follow the
internet safety guidelines at Usborne Quicklinks.